# THE TORTURED TRAIL

A Jack Ballard Novel

LINELL JEPPSEN
JEB ROSEBROOK

WOLFPACK
PUBLISHING
— EST 2013 —

**The Tortured Trail:**
**a Jack Ballard novel**

Linell Jeppsen
Jeb Rosebrook

Paperback Edition
Copyright © 2019 Linell Jeppsen, Jeb Rosebrook

Published in the United States by Wolfpack Publishing, Las Vegas.

Wolfpack Publishing
6032 Wheat Penny Avenue
Las Vegas, NV 89122

wolfpackpublishing.com

Paperback ISBN 978-1-64119-563-8
eBook ISBN 978-1-64119-599-7

Cover art: Frederi C Remington "A Dash for the Timber", Public Domain

Library of Congress Control Number: 2019933350

*In Memory of Jeb Rosebrook*

# THE TORTURED TRAIL

## Prologue

THE BLUE SASH SOCIETY MET DOWN BY A CREEK THAT meandered through a thicket of Jack Pine and mesquite a little after midnight. Torchlight flickered fitfully in the scrub, casting long, eerie shadows as the men gathered in groups of two and three. By 1:00 a.m. the assassins were assembled, and the meeting commenced.

As always, a rare bottle of Old Forester's Kentucky bourbon was produced and passed around before the meeting officially began. This was not in celebration. Rather, the strong spirits were used as a tool to unite their brotherhood once again against those they perceived as traitors to their cause.

This cause-amongst many—was the eradication of all members that had ever betrayed Quantrill's Raiders, the Regulators or their affiliates. Recently, an informant had spotted one of their *Most Wanted* heading toward the raucous town of Bandera, Texas.

One of the acknowledged leaders of the Blue Sash Society called the meeting to order, and a hush fell over the men who had reported for duty. Another leader studied a wad of papers in his hand, looked up and said, "You two! Come forward."

Two of the men who had arrived late but together moved their horses slowly toward their leaders. It was a cool Texas night but both men had tied their jackets to their saddle bags and rolled their sleeves up to display the tattoos on their inner-forearms which read, 8211863. The men surrounding them tucked their chins or touched the brims of their hats in respect of those numbers as they passed.

Coming to a creaking stop, the two men sat slightly hunched in their saddles but prideful, sensing they had been picked for a special task.

Immediately, the man with the papers in his hand said, "You two are dogging the Bandera area, right?"

Nodding, the riders murmured, "Yes, sir," and "As ordered, sir."

"Good," the leader replied. "We finally got some action coming in, and you men will be taking point."

The older of the two riders, Conrad Drago, a grizzled veteran with wiry gray hair and deeply-bracketed, down-turned lips asked, "Who we goin' after, boss?"

The undisputed leader of the Blue Sash Society, who had sat silently until now broke into a grin. "That sumbitch, Jack Ballard, that's who!"

A stir of excitement rippled like electricity through the gathered crowd. Not only was Ballard a sworn enemy, he was a thoroughly dangerous man. Going after him was akin to hunting a wounded and angry big boar Grizzly. Smart, easily provoked and deadly, any man who went after Ballard would have a fight on his hands.

Pleased as punch, the older man tipped his hat and said, "To the job, sir."

Tyson, his partner and little brother who had stringy blonde hair and cold gray eyes said, "Be our pleasure, sir."

One more bottle of Old Forester's was produced, and the men took their turn at it, until the meeting broke apart and the gathered crowd dissipated into the darkness, leaving only one witness. A rattlesnake had slithered up onto a cool rock earlier that evening and was forced to freeze in place and in clear view lest it be detected by its sudden company.

A stickler for not leaving witnesses behind, however, the leader of the Blue Sash Society arrested his horse's forward movement, turned around, rode back approximately fifty feet and pulled his pistol, turning the reptile into nothing but a moonlit spray of bloody hide.

Then, grinning in triumph, the man spun his horse around and dug his rowels into the horses' underbelly, making it cry out in pain. But it ran hell bent for leather and its rider caught up to his partner in no time, leaving only one startled coyote behind to howl at their passing.

## Chapter One

JACK BALLARD COULD HEAR THE TOWN OF BANDERA, TEXAS, long before he clapped eyes on it. The sound of bellowing cattle rang through the prairie, and the muted calls of men, horses, dogs and a smithy shaping all manner of metal goods filled his ears and he grinned.

It had been a long, hard haul from the Big River area through torrential rains and tropical wind storms that eventually turned into a baker's oven with temperatures in the high nineties and scorching winds that lashed his body dry and drove his buckskin gelding, Rebel, crazy with thirst.

Now, approximately two miles outside of Bandera, high humidity had fallen over the land bringing clouds of gnats, skeeters and biting horse flies. Jack grimaced and plucked his sweat-soaked hat off to wipe greasy perspiration from his forehead, but just as he was fixing to clap the low-brimmed hat back on, Reb let out a squeal and set to crow-hopping in place, nearly unseating his rider in the process.

"Whoa! Whoa, Reb, settle down!" Jack murmured quietly as his horse shuddered and shook. Looking down, he saw a bright red welt rising up on Reb's right wither and couldn't blame the horse for the little rodeo. He himself had been the beneficiary of a number of those damnable horsefly bites and he cursed under his breath, as Reb quieted and continued forward toward town.

Jack pulled some soothing ointment from his saddlebag and smiled slightly as he put the foul-smelling concoction on Reb's painful bite. He was daydreaming about a long, warm bath, a cold drink and maybe, the soft fragrant arms of Sally Cline, who worked at Bill Donegan's Pool Emporium.

Those things were definitely in order and... a hot meal! Donegan was the owner but he was also the head cook and specialized in big, rare beef steaks and piles of fried potatoes which he grew fresh behind his saloon.

Mouth watering slightly, Jack gazed ahead at the town and realized it was now partially hidden behind clouds of thick dust which rose into the air above it like a storm front. The smell of sweating, dusty cattle and manure had intensified as well, stinging Jack's nose and making his rising appetite diminish in a slight wave of nausea.

Suddenly, the winds shifted a bit, the dust cleared, and Jack stopped his horse and sat staring in open-mouthed amazement. The actual town of Bandera wasn't all that big, but cattle, drovers, cowboys, horses and hundreds of people swarmed across the land stretching as far as the eye could see.

The streets were alive with activity. A carnival atmosphere prevailed, and small tables and booths were set up on both sides of the road. They were filled with sundry items for sale like lumber, foodstuffs, clothing, medicines, and booze. Services were also on offer like barbers, dentists, blacksmiths, priests and even what appeared to be a small brothel on wheels. Jack grinned with delight.

He had come to the right place. There was a big cattle drive heading north into Dodge City on the Western Trail, and he was looking for a job. Thinking to get a bath and a good meal before talking to one of the head wranglers about possible employment, he steered his horse to the left and hugged the boardwalk to avoid running over or colliding with the multitude of people and animals milling about the streets unchecked.

After a couple of near-misses, and soon after pulling Reb back and away from a bar fight which had broken-out and spilled into the street nearly under the horse's hooves, Jack saw the sheriff's office and a big, heavy-set man bent over double checking his horse's shoes.

Jack steered Reb to the right, thinking to introduce himself to the local law, but his horse hadn't taken three steps when it was bowled over and Jack flew through the air, landing hard on the left side of his body.

He was smarting, but Reb was squealing in fear and Jack jumped to his feet and ran over to where his horse was disentangling itself from a big roan. Heart pounding, Jack saw that Reb was more frustrated than hurt, and he bent over, grabbed the reins on its bridle and helped Reb to his feet.

The other horse stayed down though, and Jack felt his fury grow as he studied the blood trickling from its nostrils and what looked like a bruised and swollen right front foreleg. Turning around, he glared at the young, freckle-faced boy who had run himself and his horse into them.

"What the hell, boy! You just about killed us both and it looks as though you already done in your horse. What would cause you to be so careless?" Jack snapped.

The boy whipped off his hat with a shaking hand, and piles of long red hair spilled out from under it. "Sorry, Mr. … that hoss got his teeth in the bit and wouldn't let go. I didn't mean any harm to you and yours, though. I was making for Sheriff Power's office. Comanches are running around north of here, settin' fire to one and all! They already fired my grandparent's ranch… and I… I…"

The young girl's brown eyes filled with tears, suddenly, and Jack felt his heart twist with sympathy. It had been a while since he'd lived under threat of an Indian attack, but they still happened on occasion, and no one wanted to be in their way when it did.

Watching as Reb made a grab for some loose hay dangling from a passing wagon, he realized that the girl had done no harm to him or his horse, so there was no call to be stern. Meanwhile, apparently witness to the collision, the sheriff was heading his way with a mean scowl on his square mug.

He was accompanied by a deputy who also wore an unpleasant expression on his face and a pair of pants a couple sizes too small. Jack winced with sympathy and a barely concealed smirk as the young man pulled at his crotch and tried to set his gun belt straight, so the pistol didn't whack him directly in the jewels with every step he took.

The sheriff looked Jack over with a gimlet eye but turned to the little redhead. "Maisie, what the hell are you doing galloping down the middle of Main Street in this crowd? You trying to kill someone?"

Maisie stared at the ground under her boots and shrugged. Two tears ran down her flushed cheeks and she cried out, "Sheriff Ben, you gotta come quick! The Comanches are on a rampage. They already burnt Granddaddy's house to the ground and my pa and brother are trying to save the farm without getting scalped. He sent me into town for help!"

The sheriff blanched slightly, but immediately turned to his tight-panted deputy. "Put out a call, Floyd. We need a posse headed out to the McCallister ranch, pronto!"

Then, turning to the girl, he said, "Okay, Maisie, you done your part. Why don't you head on over to the jailhouse and get yourself some water or maybe some coffee? You can sit in the front cell and maybe take a little rest, while we gather up some help."

Maisie nodded and wandered toward the sheriff's office as Jack helped the girl's worn-out horse to its feet. It didn't seem too badly injured, just old and rode too hard for its age.

He had just stepped back from the elderly roan when the sheriff turned toward him and snarled, "And *you* can just keep on heading outta town, hear? We don't like bounty hunters around these parts."

Then, turning to the deputy, he snarled, "What are you doing here still, Floyd? Get!"

## Chapter Two

---

Jack stood silently for a moment as Sheriff Ben Powers raked him with his eyes. He'd never thought of himself as looking like anything other than what he was, a drifter, a loner trying to do good wherever he went. But he had to acknowledge that his dirty clothing, sunbaked face and arsenal might give the wrong impression.

Still, despite appearances, he would rather travel with his guns than without... he'd made too many enemies over the years to go un-heeled. He watched as Powers studied his .44-40 pistol, and the Winchester carbine sticking up from the saddle in its scabbard. Seeing the dismay on Power's big blunt face, Jack said, "I'm no bounty hunter, or gunman, Sherriff. Just rode into town looking for work on that big cattle drive. Name's Jack, Jack Ballard."

Powers looked at Ballard and grunted. He *had* been studying the man's kit and saw nothing out of the ordinary, besides that seven-inch pistol barrel. Besides, most pistol-packers didn't announce their presence to local lawmen right out of the gate. The man looked tired, hungry and honest, and Powers cussed himself for jumping to conclusions. It was a failing of his—at least the Mrs. told him so loudly, and often.

Abruptly deciding to trust the man, he shrugged and said, "Come on, follow me..." Then he set off walking toward the front of a mercantile. Once there, he started tearing bounty posters off a large piece of corkboard. "If I told old Parker once not to post these things, I've told him a thousand times!" he growled.

Jack stepped to his left and removed two or three more posters while Powers wadded the bills up and swore. Finished, finally, the sheriff strode toward the front door of the store and stepped inside. Jack could hear the man shouting at someone (apparently the owner) about him maybe having to white wash the pickets in front of City Hall if he was ever caught posting that kind of crap again!

Then, he exited the building and walked up to where Jack stood. "See what I mean? Bounty hunters and crooks go hand in hand! Too often bandits will ride into town just to get a gander at how much they're worth, and once they're here they usually do just enough bad to up their ante. I won't have it!"

The man's face had turned bright red, and Jack wasn't sure what to do or say, but Powers smiled suddenly, and added, "Sorry, I mistook you for one of them skunks."

Jack smiled, and said, "No problem, Sheriff. I do look pretty rough, I know. I was just wondering where a man might find a good bathhouse, and if you knew where the trail bosses have set up business."

Powers nodded. "Yeah, I know where they're at. Head

on down the road about half a mile and you'll find Alberto's Cantina and Livery. Old Berto makes good grub and the trail bosses have set up a tent just outside the saloon. There's also a bathhouse across the way run by Berto's wife. That outta fix you up right and proper. Now, I gotta get on and try to find and subdue those renegade injuns."

Jack tipped his hat, said thanks and stepped up on his horse. With a wave he set off down the road. He rode past Donegan's Pool Emporium with some regret but seeing the crowd of people swarming in and out the bat-wing doors, he realized his daydream of spending time with the luscious Sally Cline was probably off the menu anyway.

He sighed and prompted Reb up into a trot. He smelled his destination before he saw Alberto's Cantina, which was directly across the road from the town's main stockyard. He had apparently gone "nose-blind" since riding into town because the smell of horse and cow manure, piss, and metal took on a sudden, keen edge making Jack snort and cough.

Alberto's Cantina looked to be busy enough but not overwhelmingly so, and Jack stepped down off his horse. He looked to his right and saw a small shanty with a sign above the door that read;

**BATHS**
**Men, Women and Children**
10 cents
**Cowboys**
One Quarter

Smirking, Jack grabbed his saddlebags and glanced around once more before heading inside for a good wash.

Looking further down the road, he nodded in satisfaction. A large but torn and grimy tent was set up across from the livery. A sign out front said; **TTT Ranch.**

That's the one, he thought. The biggest outfit on the drive and the most likely to need help. With a destination in mind, Jack stepped into the bathhouse and ordered the works; a bath, a shave and his clothes laundered for a buck.

An hour and a half later, he emerged feeling a little damp but fresh as a daisy. He walked over to the livery and paid a dime for Reb's lodging for the night which included all the hay he could eat and plenty of fresh water. Then he paid for a bucket of oats, and walked over to the TTT tent, looking for the head wrangler.

No luck, though, and Jack figured it was late enough in the day, the boss man either already had all the men he planned on hiring, or he'd decided to wet his whistle while he finished the job.

The cantina was a long and low adobe building with over-turned whiskey barrels for tables, short hand-made stools and a stand-up bar along the far side. It was amazingly clean and smelled like beans and fresh tortillas. Stomach growling, Jack walked toward the back and sat against the far wall.

A young woman made her way toward him. She was quite short but beautiful with an ample figure, bright brown eyes and a heart-shaped face. Her hair was pinned back but fell in rippling, black waves almost to her knees. She took note of Jack's warm appraisal, but was suddenly slapped on the rump, hard, by a dirty-looking, drunk cowboy.

The young man seemed to be more shocked by his

actions than she was, but that didn't stop her from squealing in Spanish and giving his right shoulder a swift punch.

The cowboy squealed as shrilly as she did, and he blurted, "Sorry, Ma'am... sorry! Don't know what came over me!"

She studied him for a moment, then sniffed and replied, "You jus keep your hands to yourself, si?"

The youngster blushed red, and mumbled, "Yes, ma'am. Sorry..."

Then the woman walked up to Jack and said, "Hola, my name is Marina. My father owns this restaurant... so, what can I bring you?"

Jack answered her in fluent Spanish... "A cold beer, Marina, por favor and maybe some of your beans?"

She nodded and smiled, "We have frijoles with beef tonight, senor, and fresh tortillas. Is that okay?"

He grinned, and answered, "Perfecto! Thank you."

She returned his smile and said, "I'll be right back with your cerveza..."

Jack watched the lovely lady walk away for a moment and then sat back with a frustrated sigh and studied the crowd.

## Chapter Three

TWO COWBOYS STANDING AT THE BAR STARTED SLIGHTLY and glanced toward the Spanish-speaking customer seated at the back of the cantina. They hadn't noticed him when they came in as the man was engulfed in shadow, but they recognized his voice and grinned. Their smiles were not pleasant.

The Drago brothers had ridden into town earlier that day. Although they were heavily armed, they had taken off their regular garb and dressed in the scruffiest cowboy clothes they owned. They wandered the busy streets and had also visited one of the local whorehouses, to the dismay of the working ladies they used... hard.

Once finished, Con and Tyson meandered through the impromptu fair and spotted a deputy mincing down the boardwalk in their direction. Seizing the opportunity, Conrad hailed the man with tight-fitting jeans, "Howdy!" he said. "You wouldn't happen to know if a bounty hunter named Jack Ballard has come to town? Brown hair, and kinda hazel eyes? He's a friend of ours and we're supposed to meet up with him here in Bandera."

The deputy, Floyd Davies, paused and adjusted his new jeans which had shrunk two sizes the first time his ma had washed them. He'd heard Power's words to that Ballard guy before he was sent off to muster a posse and was dismayed.

His boss was his idol, but lately he'd found himself disagreeing with the sheriff's outlook on things. Power's first instinct was to hit first-ask questions later, and he often said, "Better safe than sorry," even after he'd clocked an innocent bystander.

Floyd often thought the sheriff's actions too hasty and figured that men who had sworn to uphold law and order should act a little less like common crooks, rather than bigger and badder than most of the bad guys! He believed that a good "talking-to" worked just as well and was a lot less bloody.

Also, Floyd thought that bounty hunters were a God-given gift for regular, star-carrying lawmen like himself. He figured *his* job was to serve and protect the folks in his own town—and leave the dirty work and traveling all over God's green earth to those men who were paid good money to do so!

He just couldn't figure out why Ben hated them so and treated them with the same disrespect as any outlaw. That was why he'd been happy enough to leave when Powers had insulted the newcomer—who seemed like a keen customer but a decent guy.

He hadn't stuck around long enough to hear Jack's denial of being a bounty hunter, so he had no idea that Con's declaration was a falsehood. He studied the dirty, middle-aged man in front of him and decided to circumvent his boss' orders by being friendly and helpful. It didn't hurt that Ben had already left town to chase down those uppity injuns.

He scratched the thin brown hair under his hat for a second, readjusted his dungarees, and replied, 'Yeah, I know who you are looking for."

Both Conrad and Tyson grinned at the young idiot and Con asked, "D'ya know where we can find him? Time is, as they say, of the essence…"

The deputy nodded, "I think the sheriff sent him down to the cantina. That's Alberto's Cantina down by the stockyard. Serves good food…" But his words died as the men abruptly turned on their bootheels and strode away. *Well*, he thought. *That was rude!*

For a moment, his pride was too stung for Floyd to think about anything other than his own hurt feelings, but then common sense took over, and he felt a chill of alarm. Men like that—men with cold, gimlet eyes and grim purpose were to be handled with extreme care. But he had been careless, and in a defiant mood toward his boss— whom he admired.

Floyd turned around and started following the two men at a cautious distance. If he *had* just set two deadly hounds on an innocent man, at least he could report what had transpired to Ben Powers, once he rode back into town. Of course, there was no need to explain that he was the one who'd set the exercise in motion, was there?

─────

MEANWHILE, Jack had just been served a meal of beef and

beans with a stack of fresh fried tortillas and was setting to with good appetite. A cold beer had arrived with his meal and now Marina was flying around the suddenly busy cantina. He couldn't help but notice her grace and economy of motion as she served the cowboys and rough-necks hooch and food.

Her father and another young man were also very busy at the bar and didn't notice when one of the men at the bar grabbed her arm as she walked past with a heav-ily-loaded tray of bottles and glasses. She was concen-trating on her work and unprepared for the sudden stop, so the tray flew forward sending the glasses, beers and two whiskey bottles smashing to the floor.

Then, as if to add insult to injury, the man who had grabbed Marina's arm, slithered behind her and started fondling her breasts from behind. She shrieked in alarm and anger, but Jack had already stood and drawn his pistol.

Suddenly a hush fell over the crowd as the would-be rapist saw the heavy pistol aimed at his head. Marina scrambled backward out of the line of fire, and Jack moved his body sideways to take aim and make his large form less of a target.

Unfortunately, the man grinned with delight and squared off as well, his right-hand hovering over his own pistol. Jack's vision narrowed, and time seemed to slow down as he realized the man was probably a professional gun-slinger. That complicated things a bit.

The bar patrons backed up and crawled behind the whiskey barrel tables, preparing to watch an unantici-pated gunfight. Alberto, seeing what was about to happen, started yelling for the men to stop and take their fight outside, but the gunslinger's voice carried over the panicked owner's hollers.

"Sure you want to meet your maker today?" he hissed.

Jack answered, "You first…"

Then, quick as a snake, the gunslinger drew his pistol and fired.

## Chapter Four

BEFORE JACK COULD CHECK HIS BODY FOR BULLET HOLES, the gunslinger collapsed on the floor in a pool of his own blood. Shocked, he turned around and stared at two men who were standing in line in front of a long table with a small hand-written sign that read,

**TTT**
**Cattle Drive**
**Sign-up**

Two men stood in line and both held smoking pistols in their hands. One man was older than the other by a couple of years and had graying, brown hair and a drooping handle-bar mustache. The other man resembled his companion, but he was younger, better-looking and had a mane of light blonde hair.

*So*, Jack thought, *brothers just saved my bacon!* Suppressing the belligerent goose that had just walked over his grave, Jack glanced once more at the dead gunslinger, then moved toward the men who had shot him dead.

Holding out his right hand, Jack walked up to the men and said, "Thanks. He was a lot quicker with that pistol than I figured. You just saved my hide, and I owe you one."

Con grinned and answered, "Oh, I think you had the drop on him. We just wanted to make it a sure thing. My brother and I have been keeping an eye on that pup all afternoon. Seemed to us he was just itchin' fer a fight and he's been causin a ruckus all up and down Main Street. Came as no surprise that he decided to draw on you."

"Well," Jack sighed, "thanks all the same." Glancing up and down the line of men, he asked, "So, this is the TTT drive? I was hoping to sign-up."

"Yeah, well, you come to the right place. Listen, why don't you scooch in next to us? Looks like the hiring is almost done," Tyson offered, as he stepped aside to let Jack stand next to them in line.

A small whine of outrage came from one of the men standing behind them in line but seeing how well the three men handled their guns, the complainer didn't protest overmuch.

Jack watched as the dead gunman was dragged outside the bar by his heels and pondered the irrevocable nature of life and death, as he always did whenever someone in his vicinity succumbed to the Grim Reaper. One second a man was standing there—as big and bold as life itself, and the next second his body was nothing more than an empty husk.

Before he knew it, his whole body began to tremble as his mind acknowledged the close call. Scowling fiercely, Jack endeavored to still his nervous tremors, but Con noticed. "Enough to give a man the willies, ain't it?" he murmured but seemed kind enough, so Jack took no offense.

Instead, the older man's comment put some steel in his backbone and Jack faced forward with calm eyes.

———

Tom Orr, owner of the Triple T (which stood for Tom, Texas and Tennessee), had watched the bloody exchange with keen interest. He had signed-up plenty of cowboys, cooks, cook-hands, horse-wranglers and drovers today and was fairly pleased by his new hires. The only thing he lacked now were men who were better than average with a gun.

This was his first big cattle drive and the first time the Orr family had been able to drive such a large herd from the Rio Bravo to Dodge City. His herd was 3,000 strong, including over a thousand beeves belonging to his friends and neighbors, and he wanted to be more than certain his investment was protected against all comers.

Tom had done this kind of work all his life and knew that a herd his size was prone to heavy attrition; malnu-trition, thirst, drowning, and injury. Mainly, however, a herd this big suffered the most from theft. No matter how many men you had on hand to keep an eye out, thieves would and often did ride in after dark and make off with small, stray herds. It was a simple fact of life, but he had scrimped and saved enough cash to hire the very best to ensure his herds' safety.

Tom watched as the three men stepped up to the table

and he said, "Lookin' to head out on the trail with us tomorrow?"

Con spoke first. "Yessir. We're looking to sign-up. You still need good men?"

Orr scratched his head. "Well, I got most of the cowboys hired already, but I *am* looking for a few good pistol-men."

Con and Tyson glanced at one another and smiled. Often, besides the trail boss and their most trusted men, and the "Night Hawkers", most trail-hands were asked to surrender their firearms for the duration of a drive.

Too many strangers packed together, too soon after the Civil War, and not knowing who had fought for whom, sometimes led to violence. A fist fight was tolerated, but gunplay was not.

So, being asked to carry their guns as security was just the opportunity the Drago brothers were looking for. Conrad smiled and said, "We're yer men, then, boss. Both me and my little brother can shoot the eye out of a jackrabbit runnin'."

Orr nodded, pleased. "Good, you two will be doing most of the "Night Hawking", and you can sign your names or make your marks here on this sheet. How 'bout you?" Orr asked, turning toward Jack. "Looks like that young scamp almost got the drop on you."

Jack shook his head. "Nossir. I had him by a couple of seconds, at least. It's just that these boys beat me to it," he answered truthfully, and with certainty.

Orr nodded in agreement. He'd figured pretty much the same thing. The speed with which the tall, handsome man in front of him had pulled his revolver was nothing short of spectacular. "Okay, you three are hired to be my security detail. I know that Night Hawking is hard, and I *do* have a couple of other men who can spell ya, but that will be your main duty. You okay with that?"

The three new hires nodded in agreement, and Orr scribbled a dollar-sign and a number on a piece of scratch, handing it over for the men to study. He said, "A dollar a day, is what you'll be paid."

All three men raised their eyebrows and whistled softly, as Orr grinned. "I pay well for services rendered. Do a good job on this drive and that'll be your bonus, alright?"

"Yessir!" Jack, Con and Ty answered.

Orr grinned. "Okay then, show up no later than 5 a.m. or we'll be leavin' without you."

## Chapter Five

CURLY BUCK, TOM ORR'S RIGHT-HAND MAN, MOVED THE sign-up sheet toward the Drago brothers and studied the three new hires. He didn't care too much for the brothers —seemed to him they had shifty eyes and the kind of sly grins that spoke toward ill intentions. The other man, though, seemed like a game hand and would obviously be handy in a gun fight, which for some uncanny reason, seemed necessary for this particular drive.

Buck, who had spent much of his younger years as a Texas Ranger, had developed a keen sense of danger and impending doom. Some of that stemmed from hard-learned lessons he'd been taught during his stretch "rangering" but most of it came from simple experience.

And, he had the scars to prove it. Although still a decent-looking man at thirty-six, with a short but muscular frame, dark hair and blue eyes, he was covered on his left side from hip to eyebrow with burn marks sustained in a "to-the-death" fight with a young Comanche brave.

The Comanche chief who held Curly and two other young rangers prisoner, had pitted him against their best fighting brave for a chance at freedom. For a few minutes Curly thought his days on earth could be counted in seconds. He had given as good as he got, but he was stabbed, sliced and received third-degree burns when they'd rolled through a cookfire and the brave held him down onto the hottest coals while trying to take his scalp.

He had won his freedom and that of the other two rangers after seizing the young Indian's battle ax and ending the fight for good, but not before paying a steep price. He came close to dying in the days that followed and would display those battle-scars till his dying day.

Curly's blue eyes shifted as Sheriff Ben Powers entered Alberto's Cantina with a roar of displeasure. "Who put that dead carcass out on my street?"

Silence fell over the crowd, and Alberto started to explain the situation, but Power's gaze fell on Jack Ballard. "YOU!" he hissed, pointing.

Jack almost looked behind him to see if the sheriff's ire was directed at someone else but gave up that notion when Powers and two of his deputies made a bee-line in his direction. Next thing he knew, the sheriff had his big .44 pointed at his head.

"I'm taking you to jail for the murder of an innocent man… and for being a lying piece of shit!" he hissed.

Jack had no idea what the man was going on about but wasn't about to argue with the mouth of that hungry, black gun barrel making a target on his forehead. "Okay, Sheriff," he said. "I'm coming along peaceable."

Con shouted. "Sheriff, this man is innocent of any crime. It was me and my brother who done the deed. But, ask anyone… the pup was molesting that gal over there, and Mr. Ballard was just defending her honor. That's when the boy pulled his pistol, I swear!"

Powers, who'd been told by Floyd that Ballard was actually a bounty hunter, let his aim drop a little, and stared at Jack with cold eyes. "Is that true, Ballard?"

Jack nodded, "That's the gist of it, Sheriff."

The sheriff turned and asked Marina, "Is that true, honey?"

She glared and answered, "Si, Sheriff, ees true."

"Well, that don't excuse your lies," Powers grumped, turning to face Jack again.

Jack frowned in bewilderment. "What lies are those, Sheriff?"

Powers, whose pride had been wounded when Floyd informed him of Ballard's falsehood, snapped, "That you wasn't no stinkin bounty hunter! I told you, I won't tolerate bounty boys in my town!"

Jack's expression told Power's that Floyd's information was incorrect (as usual), and he sighed.

Jack shook his head. 'Sheriff, I told you, I'm no bounty hunter… just a man looking for honest work."

The Drago brothers kept their own council, having just signed on to the drive. Most cattle men didn't much like bounty hunters on their teams, either, and they didn't want to lose their new jobs.

Finally, the sheriff said, "I want someone to load that corpse up on a wagon and take it on down to the doc's office. Then, I want you three out of my town at first light. You hear me?"

Jack and the Drago brothers nodded in agreement, and the sheriff and his lawmen exited the bar. The Drago brothers made a hasty retreat as well, but Jack went and stood at the bar for a few moments. Glancing over to Marina, he asked, "You okay, miss?"

She smiled. "Si, senor. I'm hokay... just mad is all."

He shrugged. "Can't say as I blame you. Can I have one more glass of whiskey, please? Then, I'd better find a place to sleep."

Marina said, "Uno momento, por favor..." she walked over to where her father, Alberto, was quickly supplementing the customers glasses after the excitement. They spoke for a few moments as he filled a fresh glass with Jack's whiskey. Then Alberto glanced over at Jack and gave a sight nod.

Marina walked back to Jack and said, "Mi papá say you can sleep in our barn. It's clean and warm... besides, with all these people in town, I doubt there's a hotel room available. You want that?"

Jack, feeling the day's events catching up to him said, "Si, Marina. That sounds muy bueno... gracias."

He downed his drink in one swallow, put his hat on his head and headed out to the door. Stopping by the corral for a moment to scratch Reb on his forelock, he thought, *between land-grabbing bastards, and suicidal gunfighters, I'm more than ready to keep cows company for a while. At least it'll be quiet.*

Then, he grabbed his saddle bag and a blanket, stepped inside the barn, climbed the stairs up to the loft and was asleep within minutes.

## Chapter Six

HAVING FILLED HIS QUOTA FOR HIRED MEN, TOM ORR AND his second in command, Curly Buck, finished their drinks and headed up the street to The House of Fortune. Tom didn't care much for the place, but he knew his friend Curly had fallen in love with one of the establishment's prostitutes—a young woman named Consuela Romero.

Tom figured Curly could spend time with the girl and work the kinks out of his body while he himself enjoyed the owner's selection of fine brandies. After all, he reasoned, it would be a while before they hit Dodge City with a lot of lonely, rugged miles between here and there.

As they entered the parlor house, Curly looked toward the back of the room and spied Connie standing behind the bar, serving drinks to their few customers. The House of Fortune did not rake in the customers like the town's three other saloons, but they did a brisk, back-door business selling potions, whores and prognostications to the more superstitious citizens in the vicinity—of which there were many.

Looking up as if sensing his presence, Consuela smiled when she saw Curly staring across the room at her. She spoke a few words to the madam, who sat on a high stool behind the bar, and Curly saw the old woman nod with a slight frown.

He understood that Connie often let him sample her services for free and decided to have his fortune read tonight by the owner's sister, Madame Fortune and pay more than usual for Connie's embraces, so she could pony-up her fair share to the madam. He knew that Connie was in love with him, as he was with her, but didn't want her to get in trouble with the owners, who took a dim view of romance over commerce.

Tom said, "Have fun, Curly, but don't take too long, eh? We need to be up and at it before dawn."

Curly nodded and watched as Connie made her toward him with a smile on her face that lit up the room. "Don't worry, boss." he murmured. We'll be outta here by ten… that okay?"

Tom nodded as he watched the exotic woman named Consuela make her way toward his friend. She was not beautiful by any means, but she was striking with dark brown ringlets, a rather long Roman nose, close-set hazel eyes, and crooked but dazzling white teeth.

He was just about to turn around and head into the back room where fine brandies, poker tables and billiards were on offer when he saw Madam Fortune stop and stare at his second with wide, wary eyes.

Her glass eye seemed to reflect dark light and her mouth drooped mournfully. She turned to stare at Consuela and shook her head as the girl threw her arms around Curly Buck's neck. Then the old woman turned and walked away. *Did I just imagine that?* Tom wondered as he made his way to the back bar.

An hour and a half later, Curly sat at Madame Fortune's velvet-covered table watching as she laid out her Tarot cards, one by one. Consuela sat behind the older woman on a stool and her cheeks, which had been pink with passion an hour earlier were now ashen and the candle-light sunk her greenish-brown eyes into pools of shadow. She was tense and silent as the fortune teller's cards revealed themselves.

"What's wrong, sweetie?" Curly asked softly.

Connie shook her head as if slapped and looked up with a sweet smile. "Ah, nothing, my love. It's probably just my imagination."

"What!" he asked again, more insistently this time. Unlike his fellow cow pokes, Curly had been around and seen far too many things to explain away the unexplainable. Some of the things he'd seen Indian Medicine men do had curled his toes more than once.

"Both of you... shush now" Madame Fortune snapped.

Curly watched as the woman's hands swept the cards up and she blew on them with some sort of mumbled command, then struck the pile three times before once again laying them out on the table. He saw then, the same fear on Connie's face that his boss, Tom Orr, had noticed earlier.

"Okay, Connie," Curly said. "Spit it out. What do the cards say?"

The young woman's eyes suddenly filled with tears. "Oh, Curly... I don't want you to go on that stupid cattle drive, okay?"

Curly stared at her. "It's my job, honey. I can't just up and quit. Tom's counting on me!"

Madam Fortune stared at him across the candle-lit table, and placed the one remaining card in her hand, face-up on the table. Curly didn't know Tarot well, but even he could see the dancing skeleton that romped on the thin cardboard, and read the word, DEATH, written under its bony toes.

Consuela abruptly stood up and rushed out the door. Curly fumbled in his pocket and found more than enough cash to pay the fortune teller well, said, "Thanks," and fled to find Connie in her room rummaging in the top drawer of her dressing table. Stepping forward, he noticed a necklace in her hand, and watched as she kissed the medallion it held and walked back to him placing the necklace around his neck.

"This was given to me by my mother many years ago, back in the "Old Country". It is to ward off enemies… and danger. Please, wear this when you leave."

Curly looked down and held the pendant up to study. The central piece looked to be a flattened triangle of silver which held the shape of an elongated eye within its confines. The eye was made of expensive-looking opal, golden in color with swirls of blue and green.

The necklace, which was lovely by itself, also sported animal teeth, tiny bits of bone, and feathers. The necklace appeared ancient—and somehow, very powerful. Looking up at Connie, he said, "This is too valuable, sweetie. I can't accept it."

He started to take it off, but the woman squealed in alarm, "No! It was given freely, and now it is *your* good luck charm. Do not discard its power, please!"

Curly sighed, and let the necklace drop onto his chest, pulled out his pocket-watch and checked the time.

Looking up at his anxious lover, he said, "Time to go, honey. Don't want to keep Tom waiting…" His words were met with a cry and a flurry of fragrant hugs. "Whoa, whoa! Gosh all mighty! I'll be back in a coupla months, okay? Maybe I can make enough money on this outfit to get you outta here. We'll set up house back in Oklahoma, okay? That's my plan, anyway."

Consuela stared up at him with moist eyes. It took every ounce of strength she could muster, but she wiped her fearful tears away, smiled and kissed Curly's cheek. "Yes, Curly, just be careful of… fast water and… and long golden tresses. It will be your doom! You stay away from that and I'll be waiting every day for your safe return."

He placed his right palm on her left cheek, traced her tears with his thumb and whispered, "I do love you, you know that, right?"

She nodded in misery and replied, "Oh Curly, I love you too—with all my heart."

Curly Buck grinned, slapped his hat on his head and stepped out of the room. Just in time, too. He saw Tom wander out of the back bar and look around for his missing "second."

Waving, Curly made his way to front of the bar and left as Consuela wept alone in her room.

## Chapter Seven

Jack was sound asleep, dreaming about a young woman named Jewel. Her wide blue eyes, lightly freckled skin, her smell... he grunted and came awake all at once, every nerve in his body on high alert.

His right hand fell instantly to his 44.40 long-barreled Colt. He picked it up and pointed it into the darkness. Meanwhile, his eyes searched the lofts shadows as hesitant footsteps rustled through the hay on the floorboards. The footsteps were soft... uncertain and he heard a feminine voice swear softly in Spanish as she, apparently, stubbed her toe on some obstacle.

He relaxed and couldn't help but grin. He was in for some company, it seemed, and he could do worse than the fiery Marina Martinez. "Hola?" he whispered and heard the young woman giggle in response.

"Hola. Dios mio, it is so dark up here! Where are you?" she called out.

"Right here, Marina, a little to your right," he answered, and the next thing he knew he had a 110-

pound, dark-haired beauty snuggled up next to him in the fragrant hay.

"I… I came to say thank you for saving me tonight," she said softly, and licked his ear. "Gracias…"

Not expecting it, Jack gasped softly and then growled with desire. This girl wasn't messing around or being coy and that suited Jack just fine. It had been a long time since he'd been with a woman and every inch of his body ached for release.

Marina must have felt likewise. In a wink, most of her clothing fell away and Jack found himself thinking, *this must be what heaven feels like…*

Their first coupling was over within a couple of minutes and they laughed as tiny pieces of hay and chaff stuck to their sweating bodies. They cleaned each other off, though, and started in again—this time, much slower.

Jack was an experienced lover, but so was Marina and this time their climax was so powerful she screamed in passion, and he let out a satisfied yell.

Panting with the after-shocks of sexual abandon, they laid together, cuddling like two spoons in a silverware drawer. Then, they both fell asleep—unaware that they had company. Both eavesdroppers had trembled with desire at their lovemaking and scowled resentfully at Jack's good fortune.

―――――

A COUPLE of hours later Jack awoke to the sound of an early rooster… a very early rooster! It was still dark outside, but Jack could tell by the slant of moonlight on the roof that the three o'clock hour had come and gone. *Time to hit the trail*, he thought with a grin.

He was short on money and hadn't been paid much more than room and board by his last employer—the mother of the girl in his dreams, Kate Swain. *That's okay, though,* he thought with a mental shrug. *That old gal had no money to spare...*

He looked down and saw Marina lightly snoring in the hay-sprinkled horse blanket he'd been using to sleep on. Luckily, she was more off the blanket than on it, so he gently tugged his bedroll out from under her and placed her discarded dress over her nude body.

She smiled, slightly, like a happy kitten, and rolled over to resume her slumber. Jack grinned in return. He would not forget her, he knew.

Then, he quietly gathered his things together, and made his way down the ladder to the floor below. Much to his surprise, he saw the Drago brothers sitting together and passing a cheroot back and forth.

Jack stood still, staring at the two men. "Didn't realize I had company... how long you boys been down here?"

Both men smiled, but it was Ty who smirked and answered, "Long enough, I reckon..."

Jack felt his cheeks flush with anger at the boy's bad manners. It was only polite to announce your presence lest you surprise your hosts, but to act like a couple of Peeping Toms was downright rude.

He had thought the brothers were okay last night, but now... Jack turned way in disgust and started to make his way outside to fetch his horse when he heard Con say, "Why, you rascal! Don't you have any sense at all? Look what you done, insulting Mr. Ballard that a-way!"

Jack heard a ruckus and turned around to see Conrad hitting his little brother repeatedly over the head and shoulders with his hat. "Con! Connie, stop it! Jeez, I'm sorry!" Ty hollered.

Jack grinned.

"Don't tell *me* you're sorry, you scamp. Tell Mr. Ballard!" Con growled.

Ty looked up at Jack and said, "Sorry, Mr. Ballard. Didn't mean no disrespect. I just got a run-away mouth sometimes, surely I do!" This was accompanied by more dusty blows from Con's cowboy hat.

Jack was too amused by now to stay angry, and he said, "Well, if you overheard something, I guess that's partly my fault. Leave off, Mr. Drago. I think your brother has learned his lesson!"

Con slapped his hat on his head with one last glare at Ty and said, "Time to head out, I think. I know that the cook has coffee going by now. Those cowboys get an early start."

"How many horses in the remuda, do you know?" Jack asked.

"More'n a hundred, is what I heard," Con replied.

Jack nodded in satisfaction. *Looks like this outfit is set up well,* he thought.

"Well, I'm ready if you are. Just need to saddle up my horse," Jack said.

"Already done it for ya, Mr. Ballard," Ty said. "I done it myself."

Jack stared at the young man for a moment, and then smiled. If Reb hadn't wanted the man to touch him, Ty would be limping by now, so the kid must have been gentle enough.

Just the same, he said, "From now on, let *me* take care of my horse, okay?" Then he turned around and stepped outside into the early dawn.

Ty nodded, and turned away, but Con stared at Jack for a long moment, screwed up bitter lips and spat into the hay at his feet.

## Chapter Eight

THE MORNING WAS CRISP AND CLEAR AND AS JACK RODE toward the cattle drive, he could hear the men and animals gearing up to leave. The cattle were lowing, and the horses whinnied with excitement. A great cloud of dust was rising in the early sunlight, and Jack spurred Reb to a light trot in order to get some coffee before it was all gone.

He needn't have worried... the two cooks had several coffee pots set up with crocks of fresh milk, honey and brown sugar. Pan biscuits were also available and, for now, jam and fresh-churned butter was plentiful. Jack had ridden trail enough to know that the butter and jam would be the first to dry-up, so he grinned, took two biscuits from the cast-iron pans and helped himself to the treats.

Taking a big bite, he grinned and said, "Good biscuits... my compliments to the cooks."

The men smiled in return, and one of them picked up an additional biscuit, slathered it in a separate jar of jam and offered it to Jack. "Huckleberry... my wife picks 'em and sends most of her jars off with me," he said. "Name's, LeRoy Smithers."

Jack tucked his bounty into the crook of his left arm and stuck his hand out to shake. "Name's Jack Ballard. I heard that this outfit is well-heeled, and knowing they hired better-than-average cooks just proves it."

They nodded politely, shook Jack's hand and then moved off to tend to their chores. Jack knew that on a cattle drive, as well as in the Army, making friends with the cook or cooks was top-priority. Making enemies with an outfit's cook could lead to all sorts of unpleasantness, not to mention a long and mainly hungry excursion.

He'd heard about one cattle drive, many years ago ... the cook was a Negro man named Amos Evans, who used his wife and two daughters as helpers and dish-washers. Two drovers—general no-goods as the story went, had eventually abducted the cook's oldest daughter and raped her.

Two days later both men and their friends had died from some sort of poison. There were five-hundred miles to go on that drive but the remaining men; from the trail bosses to the night hawks made nary a peep, as they left two men cooling under the desert scrum.

It could have been anything that put those men under, the men knew, but they were also absolutely sure that the cook had gotten his revenge. It was said that there was never such a respectful crowd gathered in front of the cook-wagon as those cowboys on that fabled cattle drive.

Jack finished his biscuits, drained his coffee cup, rinsed it and set it back by the fire's coals. Then, he walked toward the large tent he knew belonged to Tom Orr, to make his presence known.

*Boy, oh boy*, he thought with a low whistle, *this is one helluva jamboree!* There were, indeed, at least a hundred horses milling about the temporary pen, a couple dozen drovers, two chuck wagons, a blacksmith's wagon, four more support wagons and about twenty-five cowboys ready and raring to head out.

Three thousand cattle surged in the distance like a brown, black and white ocean and despite the morning's chill, flies moved in great buzzing clouds over the herd. Even as he watched, ten riders galloped toward the far-end of the herd. It was, he knew, time to roll 'em out.

He picked up his pace and stood just outside the big tent belonging to the owner and trail boss, Tom Orr. He stood there along with two small, thin men who looked very much alike. "Ah, here he is now," Orr said, and moved toward Jack. "Jack, I'd like you to meet my brokers, Timothy, and his son, Theodor Turnbull."

Jack smiled and stepped forward, "Pleased to make your acquaintance," he said.

The two small men grinned and shook his hand. "I hear you'll be doing a lot of the night-hawkin'?" the older man said.

"Yessir," Jack answered.

Eyeballing his big Colt pistol, the younger man, Theodore said, "You got much experience with that pistol?"

Jack looked away for a moment, and heard the man's father say, "Now, that is not our concern, is it, sonny? Just so long as he can keep Mr. Orr's investment as safe as possible."

Jack nodded, "That's the plan, sir."

A great clatter arose from outside the tent, and Tom Orr looked impatiently at his pocket-watch. "Well, gentlemen, the drive is moving out now, and we best be on our way. So, we'll be seeing you in Dodge City?"

The older man nodded and elbowed his son toward the tent flap. "Yessir, wouldn't miss it for the world. Let's go, sonny. We're in the man's way…"

Then the owners were lost in the rising dust, and Tom said, "You ready to head out?"

"Yessir," Jack replied and followed Orr out to their waiting horses.

## Chapter Nine

Both men mounted up and Jack looked around for Con and Ty but couldn't see them through the thick haze of dust rising from the slow, forward movement of the herd.

Tom had started moving ahead but paused and said, "Ride with me, Jack. It'll give me a chance to introduce you to some of the herd bosses and fill you in on what your duties entail."

Jack nodded and pressed his heels into Reb's belly. The horse came up into a trot, and the two men made their way to the front of the drive. It was still early so dew was keeping a lot of the dust down, but the land was so parched Jack was pleased to leave the noxious cloud of steam, sweat and dust behind for a few minutes.

No sooner did Tom and Jack bring their horses to a slow walk, six men joined them, including Curly Buck. Every man there started slightly as they spied the new bangle adorning Curly's neck. One man, an oldster with a bald head and lavish chin whiskers, cackled, "Hey Curly, what ya got there? Looks like a rooster had his way with ya last night!"

Curly frowned but couldn't disagree with old man Hasting's appraisal. Although the original necklace was lovely, the embellishments were primal and ugly. The aforementioned chicken foot dangled beneath the opal medallion and was joined on either side by matching snake rattles. Feathers sprouted north, south, east and west from the center stone and Curly squirmed from their incessant tickling's.

"You just mind yer own business, Hitch," Curly murmured softly.

To Jack's astonishment, the other boys shut up immediately and Ballard understood that Curly Buck carried plenty of salt in this outfit, despite his youth.

Tom Orr's voice filled the sudden silence. "Boys, this here is Jack Ballard. He'll be doing some security work and night-hawkin' for us. Treat him good and show him the ropes, okay?"

The "boys" nodded agreeably, and Tom went on to say, "Jack, this old coot is Hitch Potter. He's been cow-dogging most his life and will not steer you wrong if you care to heed his advice…"

"And put up with his fairy tales every night," another man interrupted and shied away as Hitch reached over and knocked his hat off. "Gawd dang it!" the hatless cowboy squawked and pulled up on his horse's reins to ride back and fetch his fallen headgear.

"And *that* is Merrill Fairweather." Orr grinned. "The boy has a big mouth, but he's a top-notch cowboy. If you need any help with the cattle that'll be the man to talk to…"

"That'll be all you can do with the likes of a man with no imagination, no sense of poetry, or of the divine..." Hitch muttered as Merrill rode up with scowl and his hat firmly screwed down on his head.

Jack grinned and listened as Tom Orr introduced three other men; Bobby Joe True—assistant cook and cowboy in training, Mateo Gonzales—a Mexican vaquero and bi-lingual interpreter and finally, Latigo; head of the remuda, and a man Jack would find was an ex-slave and the best horseman he'd ever meet.

Jack nodded a friendly greeting to each man and let himself be appraised by them in turn. As if sensing the men's unasked question about who the hell Jack was, Orr allowed, "Jack here has experience with cattle and horses, and he's no green sprout, but mainly, he's good with a gun. That's why I hired him. He'll be doing most of the security work around here, along with two other men-although they may be no-shows..."

Orr turned around in his saddle and studied the herd and the men riding the perimeter. "Dammit," he muttered under his breath.

But Jack spotted two riders coming up fast and recognized the gleam of Conchos blinking in the light of the rising sun. "That'll be them, sir, riding up now," Jack said and noticed the tension leave his boss' shoulders.

Orr sniffed and said, "Good. We needed more than one measly gun-hand. Still, I hope that those two Johnny Come Lately's aren't setting a precedent. Showing up late for the first day on the job ain't no way to start..."

Jack agreed but said nothing. Instead, he listened as Orr told him and the rest of his top men the days' itinerary. Then, Orr wheeled his horse around and rode back to check on his outriders.

"You just ask if you need anything, Jack," Potter said before riding off, and the other trail bosses followed suit. Finding himself alone, Jack turned his mount's head and rode back to where Con and Ty had settled in. As he rode up, he saw that both Con and Ty seemed angry and in an ugly mood.

Pulling to a stop, Jack said, "Glad you could make it." The words were said sincerely—as a matter of fact and with no rancor, but immediately, Ty's eyebrows lowered, and his eyes blazed hot in anger.

Jack watched the man's face, and his hand dropped toward his gun belt as if it had a mind of its own. But Con said, "Goddammit, Ty! What in blazes is wrong with ye? Can't you see that Jack was just being polite?"

Ty's face blanched and he dropped his gaze. "Sure thing, bro. Sorry, Mr. Ballard. We got a late start—my fault—and I thought fer a minute you was taking us to task over it."

Jack shook his head. "Nah," he said. "I ain't your boss, so it wouldn't be my place to censor you. I was just glad to see you show up, is all." Then he gave Reb's ribs a light squeeze, lifted his hand in a wave and rode toward where Hitch Potter was monitoring the herd.

Con and Ty exchanged glances but followed Jack as he rode toward the seething ocean of cattle.

———

JACK FELT the sun warm his face and smiled slightly at the successful acquisition of a new, good-paying job. But, had he known what caused the harsh words and anger between the Drago brothers, his gun hand would have leapt into motion with rage and loathing.

What's more, had he truly known the caliber of the men he'd decided to trust as saddle mates, he'd have slapped himself hard, and quit this job for a chance to open his eyes and screw his head on straight, before somebody got dead.

———

AFTER JACK HAD RIDDEN off to join the cattle drive earlier this morning, Bo had caught the smell of freshly brewed coffee and said to his little brother, "Wait here a minute while I fetch us some coffee."

The young man who'd helped Alberto tend bar last night in the cantina had seized the opportunity to make a few extra dollars selling coffee to the host of inebriated guests that had slept it off nearby and was doing a brisk business out on the boardwalk in front of the bar.

Con walked across the street with his and Ty's tin cups, preparing to wash the cobwebs out of his head before joining up with the herd. He drank the first cup in one hot, steaming swallow and bought a second cup to go. But when he walked up to where the horses stood, saddled and ready, Ty was nowhere to be found.

He called out, and hearing no reply looked about for a few seconds wondering where the scamp had got off to. Then, his heart skipped a beat. Con knew Ty inside and out and, fearing the worst, he threw the remains of his cup on the ground and ran into the barn where the lovely Marina lay sleeping in the upstairs loft.

He ran up the ramp and, sure enough, saw his little brother standing over the girl with his pants down around his ankles and his "little buddy" grasped firmly in his right hand. He was apparently working himself up to rape Marina in her father's own barn!

Gulping, Conrad ran as quietly as possible and grabbed his brother around the middle, pulling him back and away from the slumbering beauty. Ty struggled mightily at first, but after receiving two swift punches to his kidney's, gave up the fight and stumbled back down the ramp, breathing hard and gagging at the pain that had suddenly over-taken his lust.

Con hauled his little brother outside, slapped him across the face and snarled, "What in tarnation were you thinking? Didn't you see that the sheriff here knows—and likes—that Mexican barkeep and his daughter?" Smack!

"What, did you think to be a raping her and get away with it? And what do you think would've happened if she fought back? Were you just going to kill her and ride off without a care in the world?" Smack!

Then, overcome with rage, Con yanked his hat off his head and started beating Ty with it as hard as he could. The younger man was not being hurt overmuch at his brother's swipes, but he was still nauseated by Con's kidney punches.

Ty staggered away and bent over puking, which allowed Con to catch his breath and get his nerves under control. "Come on, idiot, we have to catch up with the herd…"

"Don't call me an idiot!" Ty spat.

Con's face turned red and he answered, "I'll call you

anything I damn-well please! What you just did… it could've ruined everything!"

Ty knew this to be true and had no real answer to account for his behavior, but those sounds of sexual pleasure he'd listened to last night had triggered a primal need —not only for sexual release, but a need for revenge over the traitor, Jack Ballard.

That betraying son of a gun and his infernal good luck —his high and mighty attitude-the women who followed him around like cats in heat—the way he seemed to command respect where ever he went… it was maddening!

Still, his big brother was right… he'd almost let his impulses ruin the plan he and Con had cooked up—the plan that not only meant turning Ballard over to the Blue Sash brotherhood but taking their cut of Ballard's bonus money when this dog and pony show/cattle drive wound down.

Shaking his head, Ty said, "Okay brother, you're right and I'm sorry. Don't know what came over me."

Con just shook his head, spat and rode out at a quick trot, leaving Ty to catch up despite the throbbing pain in his kidneys.

## Chapter Ten

NOT TOO MUCH HAPPENED THAT FIRST DAY—IT TOOK UNTIL early afternoon just to get the herd moving out in the same direction. As usual with young steers, one animal after another vied for supremacy which meant that even after the herd was sorted and moving together as one—a dominant steer would buck, cut out of line and attempt to commandeer a handful of like-minded rebels with him in his escape plan.

They never got too far, but havoc usually ensued in that section of the drive as the cowboys and their horses attempted to assert their authority, and the maverick steers were rounded up and placed back in line. Older cows were worse. Acutely possessive, many of the old range cows would get aggressive if they sensed their territory was being threatened.

While steers would roll their eyes and snort but ultimately skedaddle when a cowboy and his mount drew near—an ornery old cow would often turn sideways, face-off and charge the incoming threat, which had been known to cause many a horse-wreck.

There were plenty of talented horsemen available on the plains since the Civil War ended, including freed slaves, Confederate cavalry soldiers and Mexican vaqueros but some of these same men were terrified of range-wise, matronly cows who thought every calf in the herd belonged exclusively to them.

So, those men opted for the remudas, or went on to join-up with other more westerly cavalries just to avoid tangling with a savage cow who'd got it in her head to fight. These unruly females, despite their sex, had hooked horns just as long and savage as any "Boss" bull and were often twice as mean.

So, although this cattle drive got a slow start, it was because Tom Orr wanted his most experienced and gentlest drovers to gather the herd together—safely and silently. Although the herd itself was a seething mass of noise; for some reason the riotous bellowing, low bawling, hoof beats and constant ruckus was a comfort to them. But bring in a horse or the sound of a human voice and all bets were off. It was worth the wasted hours to gentle the old range cows into line rather than spoil the goods by forcing the issue.

Jack spent most of the morning jollying the cows, heifers and steers into a reasonable formation and around 2:30, Tom Orr rode up and said, "Hey, better go ahead, get a little supper and some shut-eye so you're awake for tonight's night-hawking. The cooks are set up about five-miles north of here."

This wasn't a polite offer, but a command so Jack nodded, tipped his hat and rode to the front of the drive.

Looking ahead into the distance, he could see a line of faint gray smoke rising into the air from what looked like a large scattering of trees to his right.

He brought Reb up into a light trot and a half hour later finally reached the three wagons parked under a copse of Quakies. He could see several low-burning cook-fires and smell the fragrance of charred beef in the warm air. His stomach growled, and Jack grinned. There was something to be said about night-hawking—often the "Hawkers" got the best and freshest of whatever grub was on the menu.

He knew that the herd was, at least, five or six miles behind them and by the time the cowboys got into camp for dinner the biscuits would be hard as rocks and the steak tough as leather. *Oh well,* he thought with a shrug, *at least they would be bedded down and snoozin' with the angels rather than riding out alone in the dark of night, like me, with nothing but scorpions, wolves and Song-dogs for company.*

Gazing about, Jack noticed quite a few folks at camp—more than he'd realized earlier. There was a wagon set off under the trees and he could see great clouds of steam billowing out of deep, cast-iron vats. He could smell harsh lye soap and bleach coming from that direction and understood that he was looking at a launder's wagon.

*By God, this is a first-class outfit!* He approved silently.

Suddenly starving, Jack headed over toward the chuck wagons for some supper.

## Chapter Eleven

THE SUN HAD SET, AND DUSK SETTLED IN WHEN JACK stumbled out from the back of a prairie schooner which was specifically designed to accommodate the night-hawkers. It held two bunks on either side, a narrow table and a small set of shelves for the occupants' belongings.

He had not slept well but he was unaccustomed to going to bed so early (4:45 this afternoon after a good dinner of beef stew and yeast biscuits with cherry jam.) Still, he'd half expected it and knew that sleep would come easy by the time his shift was over.

Looking about, Jack saw the herd snoozing lazily about two hundred yards to his left, several small tents dotting the immediate area and quite a few sleeping bodies tucked up into bedrolls under the starry skies. A few fires were banked down for the night, but one larger fire with several shadowy shapes sitting around it in a circle caught his attention.

"Mr Jack... over here!" a voice whispered from his right. It was the cook, Leroy Smithers, standing under a lantern next to his serving table with a sack in one hand and a steaming cup in the other.

Jack grabbed his saddle bag and walked over to where Smithers stood. "Good evening, sir." The cook said. "This here is a bag of victuals and a cup of coffee to get you started. Made the coffee fresh fer ya," the old man grinned.

"Why, thank you, Mr. Smithers. This is a treat, for sure," Jack replied and took the cup.

"You can call me by my given name," Leroy said. "If you want..."

Jack took a swallow of the thick, hot brew, frowned slightly and exclaimed, "This is delicious, Leroy... I've never tasted anything quite like it. What's in it?"

Leroy grinned, and said, "That's a little bit of coffee, a little bit of chickaree root and a taste of honey all mixed together. Works more like a syrup than regular coffee, but it'll keep ya awake and yer guts warm on a cold night."

Jack nodded, and said, "Thanks again, Leroy. I better get over to that fire and see if Mr. Orr is still up."

Smithers filled Jack's cup up once more, poured the rest away and piled rocks around and over the hot coals to douse the flames until morning. "Good night, Mr. Ballard. You be safe out there, you hear?"

Jack smiled and walked over to the large fire. Spotting Bill Eggars sitting toward the back of the crowd, Jack kneeled and whispered, "Excuse me, but is Tom here, somewhere?"

Eggars jumped slightly and clutched at his chest. "Lordy! You scared the bejesus outta me!"

Jack said, "I'm sorry—didn't mean to sneak up on you..."

Eggars snorted. "Nah, it ain't your fault, Jack. Old Hitch is telling ghost stories tonight. It's his fault for putting evil notions in my head." The big man shook his head, adding, "As for Tom, he goes to bed early. Told me and the other boys he figured you'd know what to do. Just ride out toward the back of the herd and relieve those brothers... the Drago boys, about 11:00. Curly Buck will pardner up with you then."

He consulted his pocket watch. "That's in about an hour, so you got a few minutes to finish up your brew. Yer hoss is already saddled up and ready."

Jack said, "Thanks for that. How did Reb behave?"

Eggars grinned. "Is that yer horse's name? Gave Latigo's boy fits, he did, but he took to Latigo right away. That man may not talk overmuch but he knows his horses... sings like a bird, too."

Jack stood up, murmured, "Have a good night," and wandered closer to where old man Hitch was telling a tall tale or some sort or other.

He saw that Hitch had taken his hat off and his bald dome was bright orange in the fire's glow. His eyes were shadowed, giving his face a skull-like appearance. His husky baritone voice throbbed in the still night air.

"So," he said, "how many of you have heard about the Prairie Phantom?"

"By God, here we go again," Merrill Fairweather muttered.

Hitch turned his head sharply and snapped, "Ye best pay attention to this one Merrill—it pertains to you, after all."

"What? Why?" Fairweather squeaked.

"Just listen," Hitch intoned and turned to gaze into the

fire's dying embers. Then he looked up and said, "Whal... the Prairie Phantom is a soul-stealer, that's what. Nobody knows when or where it might show up to torment a man, but almost everybody knows when one's about because the man who's caught it's attention will to lose his hat."

The men sitting around the fire stirred and whispered like excited birds, and Fairweather exclaimed, "Oh, boy. You knock the hat off my head and now I'm supposed to think a... what'd you call it? A phantom done the deed? That's rich!"

A few titters filled the air, and Jack saw that most of the cowboys were highly amused. Except for a couple of kids sitting toward the back. They were young—probably no more than fourteen or fifteen and looked like twin brothers. Both of their eyes were as big and round as the rising moon in the sky above.

Hitch held his hands up in the air and waved for quiet. "Now listen here... I ain't a pickin' on you, Merrill, I just want you to know, that's all. Once a Prairie Phantom has his sights set on a body, he keeps making a grab fer the man's hat, because it thinks that the "man" *is* the hat, see? And to the phantom, the hat represents the soul.

So, it don't matter what uplifts the man's hat... it could be a finger of breeze that carries a man's lid away, or the prick of a cactus thorn... each time the man loses his hat, he also loses a piece of his soul!"

Then, to the amazement of all but a few, Merrill's hat sailed away to land in a pool of shadow. "Aiiieee!" Fairweather screeched in fear and the rest of the men echoed his shout, but with hysterical laughter.

Jack grinned. He had seen Mateo slyly affixing a piece

of string around Merrill's hatband, and was awaiting the punchline, which was delivered in grand fashion.

Merrill, wide-eyed and shaken, accepted his hat back from the still laughing remuda boss and glared at Hitch, who stared back at him with glee. "Prairie Phantom!" Hitch hissed, and the men roared with approval.

Merrill clapped his hat back on and growled, "I'm bedding down now and… don't none of you try anything with my hat, you hear?"

General, good-natured jeers followed the young man and Jack, grinning with amusement, walked away to find Reb and do his part in the night-hawking.

## Chapter Twelve

---

Sixteen-year-old, Bobby Joe True drove the wagon a little further when he spied another decent-sized pile of deadfall ahead. Except for the rising moon, the area ahead of him was almost too dark to see, and he wanted to hurry back to the camp site in time to hear Old Man Potter tell one of his amazing stories.

His shoulders slumped, though, in frustrated disappointment. He knew that by the time he loaded up all the firewood, made it back to camp and piled the wood next to the two chuck wagons, most of the cowboys would most likely be bedded down for the night.

Bobby Joe had wanted to be a cowboy since he was just a sprout, but he was the only son of a haberdasher by the name of Clyde True. Clyde, a widower, was a good father, if a little distracted, but his only real interest lay in hats.

Hats! All manner of hats; stove-pipes, low-crowned cowboy hats, bowlers, tams, sombreros... a hat, in Clyde's mind, represented the very nature of an upright, decent man. Not cowboys or cows, or horses, dust, sweat and endless, dangerous scampers chasing bovines across the sere landscape of Texas and all the other southern states!

That kind of occupation horrified Clyde and he would hear none of his son's romanticized notions concerning the "Cowboy" life. So, Bobby Joe had grown up learning how to make hats—as stupid an occupation to him as becoming a cowboy seemed to his father.

He was a good obedient son, though, and did his father's bidding until Clyde was carried off by a fever last February. Clyde was only 41-years-old, and he'd never thought to go under at such a young age, so he'd neglected to teach his boy how to run a shop, take care of customers or do the books.

At the tender age of fifteen, Bobby Joe sold his father's hat shop to a Chicago milliner, grabbed his father's old horse and rode off to find some cowboys. He had a plump money belt comprised of the profit from the sale of his father's business, his sewing kit... he knew how to stitch, that was fer sure, a good used saddle, and sported a fancy, black low-crowned cowboy hat—which got him laughed at more often than not.

He was turned away at the first three ranches he stopped at looking for work. Although he was possessed of some skills, a keen mind and a thirst for the work, the minute most of the ranchers and their foremen learned he didn't hardly know a bull from a heifer, he was shown the door. Until he rode up to the Triple T ranch owned by Tom Orr and his family.

Bobby was saddle-sore, humiliated and starting to think maybe he should just ride on back to the town he'd left and maybe do some clerking for the town's General store. He climbed down off his horse, hobbled to the front door of the sturdy but ugly adobe-style house set close to the Rio Grande and knock on the front door.

Tom's wife, a lovely red-headed woman by the name of Evangeline, held her youngest child on her left hip and was liberally coated with flour dust. She met the tired-looking youngster at the door and said, "Take those buckets and fill 'em up, please. I'm in the middle of making bread, and just ran out of water!"

Startled by the lady's demand, Bobby said, "Yes, ma'am!" picked up the buckets and walked about twenty-feet away to where a pump spigot rose up from the ground next to four large water troughs.

He staggered back to the front of the house with the water-filled buckets and was met by Evangeline's husband, Tom, who grinned at him and said, "Who are you, now? I know most of my hands, although they do come and go, but don't recall seeing you around before."

Bobby blushed to the roots of his hair and started to stutter, "S…sir, I come looking for a job. Sorry, but I was asked to fetch these buckets afore I had a chance to ask…"

"Oh, leave off Tom! I was mistaken, thinking he was one of ours. Unlike you, I can never keep your boys straight in my mind. He's a good worker, though. Never hesitated when I asked him to fetch me some water."

Bobby didn't see the woman, but he could hear her laugh and see her husband's smile. "It's true, kid. I was watching as you rode in. What kind of job are you lookin for?

Bobby started to squirm, but he was honest when he said, "I want to be a cowboy, sir, but I don't got much in the way of training. But I'll do whatever you ask of me-fer sure. Also, I can stitch real good and cook too. My daddy —God rest him—was no cook and I was the one who kept the table at home."

Tom had hired him on the spot and although, for now, he was only a cook's assistant, one cowboy or another always took a little time every day to teach him the cowboy way. He was learning about cattle, horses, wrangling, roping, shoeing and all sorts of animal husbandry.

It was his dream coming true... if a slow one to arrive. Right now, his job consisted of washing the pots, pans, dishes and silverware, taking care of the cook's livestock, fetching wood and tending to the cook fires.

*Oh well,* he thought to himself, *at least I'm learning a new trade—and one of my choosing rather than my pa's!*

He was just finishing up gathering the wood and putting it in back of the wagon when he heard hoofbeats. Gazing toward the tail-end of the herd, he saw two men riding close to the tree line. The moon had cleared the horizon and an errant moonbeam caught the metallic glitter of steel on one of the rider's saddles.

*That's a sword!* he thought in amazement. Squinting, Bobby studied the men as best he could in the dusky twilight. Both men were older, with gray hair and long, curled mustachios. They wore some sort of sash around their waists and they came to a stop, waiting for another rider to approach.

Bobby felt a sort of terror then. It was nothing he could put his finger one, but it just seemed strange to him and very wrong that these two strangers were meeting up with someone on the drive—in the dark—away from prying eyes.

He ducked down and knelt behind one of the wagon's

iron wheels to observe the meeting. But it was over as soon as it had begun, and he watched as the two strangers wheeled their horses around and rode off into the darkness, and the hire—a man named-Drago—roughly turned his horse around and fled back to where he'd come from.

Alone again, and scratching his head in consternation, Bobby wondered whether he should mention what he'd seen to Mr. Tom or let it be? He was just a green-horn, after all.

Chapter Thirteen

FOR THE LAST SEVERAL DAYS, THE HERD HAD BEEN MOVING steadily North and East and was now coming up on the first major river crossing at the Llano, a northwest tributary of the mighty Colorado. It was starkly beautiful country with high red bluffs, Ponderosa pine, plentiful game and good fishing.

They were headed toward one of the lowest, sandy crossings. The pace was slow, both for the herd and the herders as the desert they'd traversed the last few days had been hot and sere, the cattle were foot sore and Tom Orr was paranoid and angry.

For some reason, despite almost constant vigilance, they were losing cattle every night. There had been one case of an obvious cougar attack—a constant worry for every herd on the move, but there were also unexplained disappearances, and that's what worried Tom the most.

Usually only one or two cows a week would up and vanish, but since they'd left Bandera more than forty cattle had disappeared without a trace! Orr knew that cattle tended to wander—that's what cowboys were for—but although his wranglers searched high and low every morning, those missing cattle had not been found... and that was unacceptable!

Orr was growing suspicious. Rustlers were good at stealing cattle out from under the most observant cowboys' noses, but after more than eight days on the trail, with nary a lost cow or steer found, the herds attrition rate was starting to tell on Orr and the cowboys—whose jobs existed to keep the cattle safe and sound for market.

Orr was convinced his herd was under siege by thieves, but these rustlers were true professionals, and he was starting to worry that his herd would be reduced by half, if not more, by the time they reached Kansas... which was another two to three weeks' away. He was also starting to wonder about an inside job possibly being perpetrated by the men he'd hired for security—and those men felt his hard-eyed scrutiny.

Especially Jack Ballard. For the most part, he had been teamed up with Curly Buck, who he found to be a good man besides being a tough, canny horseman and ranch foreman. He had realized, early on, that there was a deep and unshakeable bond of trust between Curly and his boss, Tom Orr and knowing he, himself, had not made off with Orr's cattle, he'd begun to look more closely at the Drago brothers.

Still, despite careful observation, Jack could find no wrong-doing on Con and Ty's part. They seemed just as puzzled and uncomfortable with what was going on as he was. The only time he'd had doubts about either one of them was the first night he'd ridden out on his night hawking duties and found Con riding back to the herd with wild eyes and his horse lathered-up and blowing hard.

"What's up?" Jack had asked that night, looking around at the calm and mostly sleeping cattle.

"Thought I saw a pack of coyotes sneaking up on the herd," Con replied. "Can't have that, of course," the man added.

"Herd seems pretty settled," Jack said. "I guess they weren't too worried,"

Ty glared at him for a moment as if he was ready to spring to his big brother's defense, and Jack sighed. He thought, *This Ty kid is always ready to jump in—over nothing!*

But Con smiled and said, "Yeah, I rode out hard for nothing. Probably not the brightest thing I've ever done, but better safe than sorry, right?"

Right…" Jack had replied and then turned in his saddle to greet Curly Buck who was riding up on them, ready to take over for the Drago brothers.

It had been a little over a week since then and Jack knew that *something or someone* was attacking the herd, despite his constant vigilance. Still, he had yet to see any wrong-doing on the brothers' part.

He was fixing to get some sleep and sat on the tailgate of the night hawker's wagon, gazing up at high, red buttes on the far side of the Llano River. Enjoying the cool breeze and the spangle of the sun rays on the water, he suddenly saw something flash by in his peripheral vision and heard the two mules pulling the wagon he rode on squeal and snort with alarm.

"Holy shitfire!" Curly shouted. "Wild hogs are getting in the herd!"

Jack had heard that wild pigs roamed aplenty in this area of Texas and knew that the two cooks had requested someone bring down a few for their cook pots. But Tom had demurred the request. Everybody knew how dangerous wild pigs were—especially the boars whose razor-sharp tusks could gut horses, mules, cattle and men with ruthless efficiency.

Jack jumped off the wagon, and shouted, "Hold up a second, Curly!" The wagon lurched to a stop and he unhitched Reb from the back of the wagon. Then, hearing an agonized screech from an all-too-human throat, Jack kicked his horse in the ribs and rode into a frenzy of blood and sorrow.

## Chapter Fourteen

*Amazing Grace, how sweet the sound, That saved a wretch like me.... I once was lost but now am found, Was blind, but now, I see.*

*T'was Grace that taught... my heart to fear. And Grace, my fears relieved. How precious did that Grace appear... the hour I first believed.*

*Through many dangers, toils and snares... we have already come. T'was Grace that brought us safe thus far... and Grace will lead us home.*

*The Lord has promised good to me... His word my hope secures. He will my shield and portion be... as long as life endures.*

*When we've been here ten thousand years... bright shining as the sun. We've no less days to sing God's praise... then when we've first begun.*

*Amazing Grace, how sweet the sound, That saved a wretch like me.... I once was lost but now am found, Was blind, but now, I see.*

LATIGO STOOD APART FROM THE REST OF THE IMPROMPTU funeral service, closer to his horses than the assembled men. To Jack, it felt like the whole world held its breath as the big Negro sang.

His bass voice rose up into the air, trembling with emotion and restrained power; stilling birdsong, arresting the cricket's constant sawing and quieting the wind in the trees. Jack had never heard such singing before and his heart was filled with awe. It was as if an angel had come down from heaven and heralded young Ian Hart's passing with the tones of a celestial clarion.

Jack gazed over at Ian's brother, Clarence (or Clancy as he was more commonly referred to) and saw great fat tears leaking from the boy's eyes as he stared at the hump of freshly dug earth that covered his twin brother's mortal remains. Tom Orr stood close to the kid, like a father would, and Jack saw the big man's hand resting lightly on the boy's back in comfort.

Bobby Joe True stood close by as well, weeping silently. He had befriended the two boys and relied on the more experienced twins for his daily training in how to be a cowboy. He had also learned to fish with Ian's gentle instruction and the look on his face now made Jack's heart ache with sympathy.

When the song ended, Latigo clapped his hat on his head and walked away to mingle with the remuda, and Jack knew the funeral service was over. He looked again at Clancy's pale face and saw Orr turn him around and walk away from the gravesite. They were making for Tom's wagon and Jack knew that, at least for the day, he and the boy would ride in the wagon rather than out in the herd, as Tom usually did.

The more Jack learned about the caliber of the man who'd hired him, the more respect he felt for Tom Orr. Rare was the man who treated his hired hands like family but could be as tough as boot leather when the need arose. Jack's own father had been like that—stern and loving at the same time—until he'd died protecting the womenfolk in his hometown from Quantrill's Raiders…

Jack abruptly shut that train of thought down lest he lose himself to a regretful past and the choices he'd made as a younger man—choices that still broke his heart and sometimes made him doubt his own sanity. He looked around for Billy Joe, thinking to offer some comfort if possible, but the kid had disappeared into a swirling cloud of dust.

So, he turned and made his way to the night hawker's wagon and saw that, for now, he was alone. Although it was high time to get some shut-eye before their shift began, Curly was still out accessing the damage those wild boars had done to the herd, the men and some of their equipment. He vowed to let Curly get a couple extra hours of sleep before rousting him for tonight's shift.

Sitting on the edge of his cot, Jack took his hat off, yanked off his boots and laid down to try and get some sleep. Still, the frenzied images of what had taken place a few hours earlier played in his mind's eye, chasing any hopes of slumber away.

———

*JACK KICKED his horse and galloped as fast as he could toward the two boar hogs which were fighting to the death over some territorial dispute. He had tangled with wild pigs before and* remembered a pony he'd ridden when he was just a spud and recalled how the poor animal had screamed in agony as another wild boar gutted it like a river trout.

Hoping to stop that from happening again, Jack rode up on a sight that took him back to the childhood memory that haunted him still. Apparently, the hogs' life and death struggle had terminated under Ian's little cow pony, and although the pigs were both dead—one from the razor -sharp teeth of its rival and the other from the round of Merrill Fairweather's rifle— both the pony and its rider were dead.

It appeared to the cowboys who'd seen what happened that the hogs were completely oblivious to the herd's presence when they'd decided to fight it out and although they were not actually attacking Ian or his mount their tusks had flashed in the sunlight like razor blades—severing the pony's legs and spilling the boy to the ground, where he'd succumbed to those same slashing tusks and teeth before he could crawl to safety.

Luckily—if you could call anything "lucky" about the incident—the herd had not been bunched-up due to their slow pace along the river. There were a hundred little herds traveling loosely together and maybe, a ten-foot perimeter around the area in which the pigs had fought.

Although the night hawker's wagon traces had broken when the pigs ran under the mules' hooves, and Ian's borrowed saddle was scratched and torn, no one besides Ian and his horse, Sally, was hurt, except for Merrill's tailbone which was bruised and sore from the little rodeo his horse had engaged in at the sight and smell of the hogs' bloody struggle.

On a normal day, when the cattle were traveling in a tightly-packed column, a stampede would certainly have ensued with the introduction of the two battling beasts. And, to a cattleman, nothing on God's green earth was scarier or more hazardous than a stampede.

Still, luck aside, Jack mourned the loss of Ian. The little carrot-top with his wide brown eyes and abundant freckles had always carried out his chores with friendly enthusiasm and a willingness to learn new things. Now, those eyes were closed for good, and Jack knew that Ian's loss would haunt his twin brother forever.

Jack grimaced, sighed and shut his eyes, trying to get some sleep for his shift later this evening.

## Chapter Fifteen

---

THE HERD MADE ITS FIRST RIVER CROSSING WITH LITTLE trouble, due to Latigo and Tom's skill in picking the right place to hit the water. On the south side of the river the water ran shallow and firm and the animals only needed to swim about fifty-feet until the north side rose up sharply to meet their churning hooves.

The sun was high in the sky and hot, so both the animals and men enjoyed getting their feet wet. The cool water also seemed to soothe the men's spirits as the death of young Ian had had a sobering effect on the trail hands' emotions. Still the mood was somber, so Tom decided to strike camp for the night by the river's northern flank.

Jack had managed to get about three hours sleep before the river crossing, but visions of the wild hogs' fight and Ian's mangled body repeatedly jerked him awake. Giving up on any more sleep, he jumped out of the wagon and told Curly to get in back and try to get some shut-eye while he still had half a chance.

Curly rubbed his hands over his whiskered cheeks and

nodded wearily. "Yeah, I'm startin' to see double." Climbing down off the wagon bench he took Jack's place in back and Jack took up the reins to join the ring of wagons which were circling around a tall ash tree.

As he hobbled the mules, after letting them stretch their legs out, he glanced up and saw Mateo staring off into the distance from which they'd come. The man's dark eyes which normally sparkled with mischief, were shadowed and the tension in his body had apparently transferred to his fine black gelding, which also stood trembling on high alert, its ears pricked to the south.

*"Eh, Mateo, mi amigo... que pasa?"* he asked the vaquero.

Mateo glanced over at Jack and muttered, *"Es nada...* I thought I saw some bad men—*mui malo banditos*, but now I do not... *es nada."* The young man shook his head and rode off leaving Jack to wonder what the young man had seen-if anything.

Deciding to look for himself, he put nose bags filled with oats on the mules in his care and mounted his horse for a short ride to the bank of the river they'd just crossed. The light was still pretty good and when Jack brought Reb to a stop, he pulled his spyglass out and scoured the countryside for Mateo's *mui malo banditos.*

South, East and West he looked, but saw nothing out of place. There were a couple of bluffs a gang could hide behind, a few Jack pines and several clumps of tall mesquite, but try as he might, Jack saw nothing but a pair of Jack rabbits bounding erratically from one hump of hillside to another.

He momentarily considered going after the two rabbits to add to the cooks food stores (donations to the communal pot were always welcome) but he knew that by the time he crossed the river, they'd be long gone. Besides, he didn't wish to get himself and his gear wet again. Although the days were bright and hot, the night-time air-cooled things down considerably and he didn't want to shiver with cold once he headed out at eleven o' clock to watch the herd.

Deciding that the Mexican was right about being mistaken, he headed back to camp and hobbled his horse. He filled one of the now empty nose bags with oats and strapped it around Reb's head. Then he walked toward the central fire to visit with the other men and grab a bite to eat.

There were a couple of poker games going on, but most of the cowboys gathered around were quiet. Jack could see old Hitch Potter scribbling in his ever-present notebook, and Tom Orr sat off to the rear with young Clancy. Looking further on and Jack could see that the cooks were keeping Bobby Joe busy.

He walked up to where Tom sat with Clancy and said, "Thought I'd ride out early tonight, Tom. Can't seem to sleep, and I figured I'd let Curly get a couple extra hours of sleep before I rousted him out of bed."

Tom nodded and said, "Good thinking, and timely too. I already asked Ty Drago to head back here early, so you could team up with Con for a few days... that okay with you?"

Jack said, "I reckon so... any particular reason for the change?"

Tom stared into the dusk for a moment before answering. "Just thought to change up the night watch for a little while... maybe see if the cattle thefts change up or stop happening." He glanced up into Jack's face, adding, "Any problems with that notion?"

"No sir," Jack smiled slightly. "In fact, I think that's a good idea."

Orr grinned back. "Glad you think so, Jack. You know my thinking on this matter, but truth be told, I never figured you for a cow thief. Still, watch your back, okay? You keep an eye on Con and Curly will be watching his little brother. We need to get a handle on what's going on, before we lose the herd altogether."

Jack slapped his hat on his head and said, "I'll head out right after I grab a bite to eat, okay?"

Orr nodded, and shook Clancy's shoulder. The kid had fallen asleep and was slumped against the big man's left side. "C'mon kid. Let's get you to bed."

Jack walked toward the cook wagons thinking that with Tom Orr's gentle guidance, maybe Clancy would recover-no harm done—from Ian's untimely death.

After grabbing a couple of cold bacon sandwiches from Hank Lemke's cook wagon, Jack walked over and grabbed his horse. As usual, Reb was raring to go. "Let's go and see what night hawkin' is like with Con Drago," he murmured to his horse who swiveled his ears back and forth at the sound of his master's voice.

Jack rode slowly to the back of the herd—he was almost three hours early, after all. But, looking ahead, he saw Ty and his horse break away from Con and trot in his direction. Moving up close, Jack saw Ty grin and say, "It's getting late! Thought you wasn't gonna make it!"

Jack decided then and there he didn't care for the younger of the two Drago brothers. Ty was joshing he knew but there was an edge, sinister and sharp, to the younger man's manner Jack just couldn't abide.

Smiling tightly, Jack tipped his hat and rode past Ty who had brought his own horse to a halt to shoot the breeze with the older man. Seeing himself snubbed, Ty glared at Ballard's retreating back and then grinned.

*Oh yeah*, he thought savagely. *You'll be getting' yours, soon enough, Jack Ballard.*

## Chapter Sixteen

MATEO GONZALES LED HIS GELDING TO THE REMUDA, SO the horse could graze and rest the night and slowly walked to his saddle and bedroll for some sleep. He was still shaken by what he thought he'd seen a little while ago in the uncertain dusk of early evening. Were those four shadowy forms just a product of his imagination or had his step-father's minions come to exact their vengeance?

Shaking his head slightly, he was startled by a horse and rider that loomed up out of the darkness almost on top of him. Thinking that certain Mexican bounty hunters had suddenly appeared like spirits in the middle of cow camp to lay him low, Mateo pulled his firearm and sighted in on Ty Drago's leering face and stringy blonde hair.

"Hey, watch it, Beaner!" Ty hissed, and spat a big glob of spittle on the ground at Mateo's feet. The man glared down at him in hostility, but quailed when Mateo cocked the hammer on his pistol.

At one time, this gringo would already be leaking the

last of his lifeblood onto the dust, but Mateo had put aside the life of a pistolero and now only wanted to live the rest of his days in peace. Watching Ty's face slowly lose color *did* give Mateo some pleasure, however.

Both Ty and his older brother, Conrad Drago, had insulted him and his heritage several times since the cattle drive had left Bandera. Never out in the open like an honest man in the heat of anger and prejudice might do, but always in secret, behind the backs of anyone in authority, like Tom Orr, Curly Buck or the new hire, Jack Ballard.

"Beano!" they'd hiss as he walked by and, "Greaser" and "Spic". Their insults seemed to follow Mateo wherever he went. Still, he had to admit those men's prejudices weren't exclusive to only him. Mateo had heard them utter worse things like "Nigger!" to the remuda boss, and "Chinkies" to the laundresses.

Mateo knew in his heart that some men were born to a life of hatred and scorn and were taught at an early age to loath and feel superior over anyone who was even slightly different than themselves. *Still*, he acknowledged, *I will not be subject to their insults any longer.*

Although he wanted to drill the smug expression off Ty's stupid face, he knew that the best thing he could do was report their abuse to the boss, Senor Tom. Although he hated to rat on anyone, Mateo resolved to do just that come morning—not only for himself but for Latigo, and the two elderly Chinese sisters that had signed on for the drive.

He holstered his gun and grinned up at Ty who was still sitting stock-still with his hands up in the air as if pinned into place by the point of Mateo's pistol. "Pardone me," the vaquero said. "I was no looking where I was going..."

Twenty-seven-year old Mateo was devastatingly handsome with bronze skin, large brown eyes and snowy white teeth. He was so handsome that many of the other cowboys who had ridden with him before kept a distance from him when entering a saloon or whore house because they knew they paled in comparison to the young Mexican man, and the prostitutes would give their wares away for free if only the dark-haired cowboy looked at them twice.

Realizing that several cowboys were now staring in his direction, Ty swallowed and said, "Hey, no problem... sorry." Then he slapped the reins on his mare's neck and trotted over to where Latigo stood watching with grave eyes.

Latigo felt the same as young Mateo, but obedience and a deep-gut instinct to obey the *White Man* had been drummed into him at an early age, and he doubted he'd ever get over it.

This did not stop him from daydreaming about pounding that scrawny Drago boy into the ground like a fencepost. Shaking his big head as he took the reins from Tyson, Latigo marveled at the kid's confidence. *Why*, he thought, *I over top him by almost a foot and must outweigh him by fifty pounds... What is he thinking?*

Mateo had walked away by now and sat on his bedroll staring off into the darkness. Casting Ty Drago from his mind, the vaquero wondered if his past had finally caught up with him.

Mateo had been born of a happy but penniless young couple from Spain who worked for a rich land owner in northern Mexico by the name of Arturo Fernando. His papa, Juan Gonzales, tended the fields and cut hay for the Patron, and Mateo's mama worked in the kitchen. His father had also helped the stable master train Arturo's fine Thoroughbred horses. It had been a good existence until Juan was kicked in the head and killed by one of the Patron's stallions.

It was a sad time, but Mateo carried on as if life knew no bounds. He did his work in the fields and garden, as ordered, but played to his heart's content with the other peasant children in the hot Mexican sunshine. Everything stayed the same until the day Arturo took his mother as wife.

Rosa, Mateo's mother, was pure Castilian and absolutely beautiful. Her long hair shone like a black bird's wing and her complexion was pale and lush. Her large, slightly slanted black eyes and ripe red lips drew the other men on the hacienda to her like bees to honey. Although she was uneducated, almost simple, her beauty was noted by all, and her lack of intelligence ignored by most.

At first, Mateo was proud of his mama. After all, her rise in situation had elevated her son's position as well. He dressed in the newest European fashion and was tutored by the finest teachers. He was taught to ride and shoot and wield a sword like a nobleman's heir. By the time he was fifteen, Mateo's handsome face, fine manners and potential wealth had attracted a long line of hopeful senoritas who were eager to take his hand in marriage.

But eventually, Arturo's passion for Rosa waned and boredom settled in as the months and years went by. Twice, she miscarried, and by then Arturo's patience with his beautiful but empty-headed wife had turned into loathing. That was when the beatings began.

Mateo ignored it for a while. His step father's daily beatings seemed harmless at first and Arturo was subtle in his attacks. But, finally Mateo had enough of seeing his poor Mama creep around the house like a wounded mouse, with blackened eyes, and split lips. She was often so hunched over with pain she looked and acted like an elderly abuela, and her silly but happy words dried up into painful whispers, if she spoke at all.

One morning as Mateo sat at breakfast, he saw Rosa peek around the corner of the dining room door and flinch with fear when she saw him sitting at the table. Hurt and embarrassed, he stood up in anger and shouted, "Why do you look at me like that, Mama? I do not hurt you—eh… come back here!"

Mateo jumped to his feet and followed his mother out into the main hallway, but Rosa fled and tried to run up the staircase to hide in her room as usual. Then, Mateo saw her fall to her knees and groan. Realizing that something was terribly wrong with the way his mother was crouching on the stairs, he flew upward, taking the stairs two at a time and bent down to help her to her feet.

That was when he caught sight of her back. Her dressing gown had only been partially fastened and the ties had come loose when she fell. Mateo gasped in shock and outrage. The skin on his mother's back was crosshatched with whip marks and was really nothing more than bloody, shredded meat. From her neck to the small of her back the skin was black, blue and purple with bruises.

Turning her around as gently as possible, she moaned

in dumb but abject terror. Mateo saw that most of the front of her body was in the same condition. To his horror, Mateo also saw that his mother's eyes looked like those of an abused dog—all trust she might have once had in the world around her had vanished and she now cowered somewhere deep in her own soul. His own mother was nothing more than a silent and witless victim of the worst case of abuse Mateo had ever seen.

A high keening rose from Rosa's throat as she stared up at her son and Mateo's heart broke into a million pieces. He picked her up and hustled her out of the main house and into his own opulent quarters, led her to the bed and told her to lie down, stay as quiet and rest.

Then, he grabbed his pistol and marched out of the house to where his step-father stood by a paddock. He was studying the lines of a new stallion he meant to purchase from a neighboring farm and turned around with a slight smile as Mateo approached, but frowned when his stepson shouted, "Patron! I challenge you to a duel at sunset!"

## Chapter Seventeen

BOBBY JOE TRUE WATCHED HIS FRIEND AND MENTOR, Mateo, as the handsome vaquero tossed and turned in the twilight. He was wondering if he should get some of his worries off his chest and confide in Mateo about what was on his mind or leave the matter alone. Bobby knew he was just a kid, after all, and not very experienced and... prone to terrors.

Thinking back on some of his sudden frights since they'd left Bandera didn't help matters much either. He was scared to death of coiled up rattlers with their nasty, buzzing tails and of the coyotes' Swan songs which jolted him awake at night. He was also frightened of the occasional Indian outrider that appeared on the horizon from time to time, only to stare down at them with cold, alien eyes.

He was determined to become a cowboy but wasn't entirely sure whether his nerves would survive the experience. Cringing, Bobby gave himself a mental slap and decided to go and talk with the man who had invested so much of his precious time in shaping Bobby Joe's future. Just because Bobby knew he was a bit of a coward didn't mean he wasn't bright, observant and game to learn new skills.

Besides, it was Mateo who had taught him that there were many dangers on the open trail and that only a fool would ignore what his heart tried to teach. And, right now, Bobby's heart was screaming at him to tell on Conrad and Tyson Drago. It wasn't just one thing that had every hair on Bobby's head standing on end, but many things combined.

First was Con's constant rendezvous with something or someone traveling behind the herd. It was his job to go and search for wood or cow chips for the cooks' fires and five times over the last eight days—just like clockwork—Conrad would wheel his horse around at dusk and ride off into the distance, leaving his brother alone to ride herd.

This, in Bobby's mind, just didn't make any sense—especially since so many cattle had come up missing since they'd left Bandera. The herd, even bunched-up was spread about 200-yards across—standing side by side—and one cowboy could not guard both sides at once.

At least, Bobby Joe didn't think it possible. The other thing that didn't add up (or maybe it really did add up) was the fact that three out of the five times he'd seen Con ride off into the shadows they'd left behind, cattle had come up missing.

He hadn't shared this intelligence with the cooks—they thought he was a cooks' trainee—and not a very good one at that. Also, he had heard them both say to mind his own beeswax and keep his eyes to the fire instead of constantly pestering the hard-working cowboys to show him the ropes.

Gazing over at Mateo, Bobby saw the man's eyes open momentarily, and he decided to go ahead and get his worries off his chest. He threw back his oilskin blanket, clapped his dirty but still handsome hat on his head and crept over to confide in the Mexican vaquero.

———

MATEO WAS DREAMING of the fateful day he had shot his step-father and liberated his poor mama from her physical and emotional abuse. He was victorious in the duel, and had spirited his mother away from the hacienda, but the cost was severe.

Arturo was furious with his stepson. He had asked, "Have I not freely given you everything your traitorous heart desires? Have I not shared my wealth with you and your ignorant mother? How dare you call me out in my own hacienda!"

What Mateo didn't know was Arturo was worried. The Patron had warned Rosa constantly to stay in her rooms and never let anyone see her body and what he, himself, had done to it. He had thought her so cowed, it never occurred to him that the maids in the house had also stopped bringing the mistress any food.

Mateo found out later that his mama was deathly afraid to leave her rooms, but her belly would not let her rest until she ate enough to keep alive until the next round of beatings began. So, she had crept down the stairs when she thought the coast was clear and was shocked to see her son sitting and eating breakfast by himself in the dining room.

She honestly believed that Mateo was aware of what Arturo was doing to her and was complicit in her torture, so she had tried to run away. But he had caught her and the shock in his eyes revealed that he was nothing more than a callow youth; self-absorbed, yes, and selfish but not evil as she had presumed.

Later, staring up at the white-washed walls of her son's elegant quarters, she had heard the shots and fearing the worst, she jumped out of bed and ran to the door to see if her nino was all right, but saw him running toward her with frantic eyes. "Mama, we must go now!"

"Go? But Hijo, I need my things!" she cried, but Mateo shook his head.

"The duel was legal and witnessed by the local federales, but the men here, they do not care. I worry that they will shoot us or hang us by the necks if we don't flee. Now, andele, Mama!

They had fled into the night with nothing more than the clothes on their backs and what little pocket change Mateo had on his person. But there was really no place to go—not for a sick and wounded woman. So, he took his mama to the closest nunnery he could find and left her with the sisters to fend for himself.

He led a life on the run for many years after that. He was good with horses, a steady hand with both gun and sword, and a canny scout. Sometimes the company he chose to keep skirted the very edge of the law, but mostly, he did honest work for a modest living.

Finally, just after hearing that Rosa had passed away, he started working for Senor Tom, and had since then gained a measure of happiness. His was not the life he had planned on having but it was honest work amongst honest men. Still, though, he kept his ear to the ground.

He had heard a while back that many of the men who once worked for Arturo Fernando were still angry at what they perceived as Mateo's betrayal. (Mateo was sure they were angrier at losing their paychecks than at his perceived lack of honor). What's more, they had convinced some of the local federales that witnessed the legal dual that Mateo was nothing more than a murderer —a patricidal maniac—and must be hunted down and brought to justice—for a fee.

Thinking once more about his poor, dear mama, Mateo heard her whispered voice calling out his name and his heart broke anew... Mateo... Mateo..."

## Chapter Eighteen

---

MATEO AWOKE ABRUPTLY AS HIS MAMA'S VOICE WAS replaced by that of young Bobby Joe True's.

"Mateo, hey, are you awake?" the boy whispered.

Grunting, Mateo opened one eye and said, "Well, I am now. What is it?"

The teenager looked embarrassed but determined in the moonlight. "I'm sorry if I woke you up, sir. I thought you was already awake, but I need to talk to you about something... I think it may be important."

Yawning, Mateo sat up and said, "Si, mi amigo, what's troubling you?"

Bobby studied his friend's face, wondering if he was doing the right thing, or risking his chances of learning how to cowboy by being a tattle-tale. Still, he plunged ahead and told Mateo what he'd been seeing the last few sunsets as he wandered their back trail in search of fuel for the cooks' fires.

At first, Mateo stared off into space as Bobby told his story and wished he could grab a few more winks... it had been a long day after all, and very sad. *Also*, he thought, *Bobby is a good boy, but he does jump at a lot of shadows.*

However, by the time Bobby finished his hesitant tale, Mateo knew that the boy's worries were serious, and not only harmful to Tom Orr and his herd but potentially dangerous for the men Tom had hired to tend his cattle.

He listened carefully and when Bobby Joe wound down, he touched the kid's shoulder and said, "It is good that you came to me with this, Bobby. The camp is sleeping right now, and Senor Orr needs his rest too. But, first thing in the morning, I will tell the boss what you have seen, okay? I am sure that those two hombres, Tyson and his hermano, Conrad, will be asked to leave-pronto!"

Relieved that his information had been well-received, Bobby smiled and said, "Well, sorry that I woke you up, but I thought someone should know." He yawned and shook his head. "I better get some shut-eye. Thanks, Mateo…uh, buenos noches, amigo," he added shyly.

Mateo grinned. He had been teaching the boy some rudimentary Spanish, thinking that if the kid was truly headed into the cowboy life, he would need at least a smattering of Spanish to deal with the many vaqueros and Spanish-speaking Indian tribes in Texas, New Mexico and the southwest territories. Nodding, he answered, "Gracias, friend. We will see you manana."

He watched for a moment as Bobby rolled himself up like a burrito and went to sleep, then he thought about what he'd heard. He didn't like those Drago men, and hated how they treated him, but he wanted to be fair-handed when he talked to Senor Tom in the morning.

Gossip was as plentiful as red beans on a cattle drive, and sometimes personal dislikes could ruin a successful trip. Perhaps he would take Bobby with him in the morning when he talked to Senor Tom. That way he could leaven the boy's excited report with more mature and somber reflection.

Abruptly, the day caught up with him, and Mateo fell sound asleep.

———

TY DRAGO'S mouth had fallen open when he heard the boy's words to Mateo, and he closed it with a dry click. He was standing nearby behind the big ash tree the camp encircled and had hidden in the shadows when the kid got up and walked over to the spic's bedroll.

Fingering the deadly sharp Bowie knife in his right hand, Ty shrugged and put it back in its sheath. He had come here to run its blade over the uppity Mexican's neck, but now it was too late.

In addition, Ty knew that his hot rage had almost gotten him, and his brother kicked off the crew, and possibly even hanged by the men in camp, when they found Mateo dead in the morning light.

Still, no man was allowed to get the drop on him without payback, even though it appeared, surprisingly, that Mateo was one of the herd bosses or he would not have been allowed to carry a firearm.

Ty was annoyed by his own shock and confusion. He had been night hawking since the drive started and usually just fell into his bedroll and slept the day away in the morning when they rode back to camp. He had, so far, paid little attention to the day-timers, and knew that if his and Con's mission was to succeed, he needed to pay better attention to what was right in front of his eyes!

Frowning, Ty wondered, *why would any white man entrust a position of authority to a Mexican beaner?* Why would Orr choose a Mexican or a black man over his own kind? Even Latigo carried a gun on his hip… a blackie with a gun! To Ty's mind, this whole outfit was crazier than a Loonie bird.

Ty knew that his sudden red rages often got him in trouble and irked his brother to no end, but was he just supposed to stand there and stare down the barrel of some Mexi's pistol? A few minutes ago, he hadn't thought so, and he'd truly meant to wet the ground with Mateo's blood, but now he was grateful for the boy's intervention.

He pulled his knife out of its scabbard as he walked back to his bedroll and studied it in the starlight, bouncing it back and forth from his right hand to his left and reveling in its balance and weight; imagining the feel of it in his hand as it sliced through a certain Mexican's jugular.

He smiled. Sure, he might have gained a momentary thrill, but tomorrow he'd have to answer some mighty tough questions and his own brother's wrath. Shaking his head, Ty knew that he was lucky. He had heard the kid's report, and knew now that one way or the other, Con needed to do something. Not only had the trail boss split them up, but the kid had apparently noticed Con's nightly rendezvous with the Blue Sash brotherhood.

For now, anyway, the brotherhood's steady supply of good beeves would be at an end, which would not be good news for their real bosses. He glared, and thought about what he could do to stop the boy and the beaner from blabbing their mouths…

"Hey, there you are. I've been looking all over for you." Curly Buck was standing in front of Tyson and looking at him with cautious, suspicious eyes.

Ty wasn't sure why at first, then he looked down at the knife in his hand and hastily put it away. "Sorry, just putting an edge on my toothpick. Is it time to go already?"

Curly nodded. "Yup, past time, actually… it's almost midnight."

Sighing, Ty said, "Okay, just give me a second, and I'll meet you at the remuda."

Curly said, "Okay, I'll be there."

Ty watched the dark-haired cowboy with the burned face walk away and wished he'd gotten a little bit of sleep instead of trying to feed his revenge, but it was too late now. Shrugging, he grabbed his rifle, drank the last of his cold coffee and set out after Curly Buck to spell his brother and that traitor, Jack Ballard.

## Chapter Nineteen

Riding out, Curly and Ty split up to meet the men who were stationed on either side of the herd. Curly was anxious to ask Jack if he'd noticed anything suspicious about Con's movements throughout the evening and Ty was desperate to talk to Conrad before morning came and Mateo had a chance to share what he'd heard about Con's movements with Tom Orr.

Although Ty was cursed with an over-abundance of rage and frequent bouts of fury, he was no dummy. He'd just remembered something he carried in his saddlebags since he and his brother visited Austin last month and watched the 4th of July parade.

He'd stepped aside as the fire trucks and rodeo cowboys passed by and told Con he'd be back in a jiff. Then, he walked down two blocks and stepped into a local Chinese apothecary. Once there, he'd purchased a little opium, some poppy-seed medicine, and a fistful of firecrackers.

He'd already partaken of the opium, (on the sly and when Con was otherwise occupied) but had given Con the poppy-seed medicine which was a necessity on long assignments like this one. After all, one never knew when a snake bite, a scorpion sting, or a fever might take a hold and the poppy could be cooked down into a pretty effective medicine.

He'd purchased the firecrackers on a whim—and for a few laughs—but now he thought of them as a diversionary tactic. He just needed to give them to Con before the other night hawkers took notice. He dug his heels into his horse's belly and heard it snort with discomfort but break into a satisfactory gallop.

Blowing up to Con's position in a cloud of dust and enduring Con's exasperated glare, Ty reached out his hand and handed a 30-inch roll of Chinese firecrackers to his brother. Staring down at the rolled-up fireworks Con raised his eyebrows, and said, "Where did you get these and what are you handing them to me for?"

Glancing about, Ty said, "Put 'em away quick, before one of those two sees us!"

Nodding, Con put the firecrackers in his coat's inside pocket and said, "Okay, calm down and tell me what's going on."

Quickly, Ty outlined what he'd heard from young Bobby Joe True, and sketched out his plan to keep Bobby and Mateo from telling Tom Orr about it and blowing their cover.

Con frowned and stayed silent as he thought about how the kid could ruin everything… then he nodded and said, "Consider it done—just make sure you're well away from the action once it starts."

Then, they heard a shrill whistle as Curly Buck rode toward the back of the herd. "Gotta go, Con," Ty said, adding, "You look sharp too, okay?"

Con said nothing but rode forward to meet up with Ballard. As he rode, he thought about Ty's plan and felt a momentary regret. He'd done a lot of heinous things in his life—mostly for revenge and honor's sake, but this was something else...

*Still*, he mused, *I have a job to do and that kid and his Mexican confidant are about to put an end to things, unless I can divert their plans.*

———

JACK BALLARD THOUGHT about his short visit with Curly Buck and regretted not being able to alleviate his and Tom Orr's fears. But, nothing out of the ordinary had happened overnight and he would be willing to bet that no beeves had gone missing either.

Of course, that fact alone could, if examined closely, cast suspicions on Con but how were they supposed to get any proof of the man's misdeeds, if he acted like nothing more than a good and capable cowboy?

Then, Con rode up to meet him with a sunny smile and said, "I'm ready for some good rack time. How 'bout you, Jack?"

Ballard nodded, and backed up his non-verbal communication with a giant, uninvited yawn. "Yup, that sounds real good to me."

Con laughed. "Wonder if the cookies are up yet? Or if they have any coffee set by?"

Jack answered, "Probably. They seem to know what they're doing, for sure."

Con nodded, and said, "Well, see you tomorrow, Jack. Is it okay with you if I take the left-hand cot?"

Jack shrugged, "Sure, don't care one way or the other."

Then Con tipped his hat and reined his horse to the right, making his way to the remuda. Jack watched him go and found himself wondering if he and the others were being too hard on the man.

Sure, he had seen Con ride off once, but that was all, and herds *did* get robbed at night whether night hawkers were watching or not. He had seen Mexican vaqueros ghost whole herds out of existence and drive them back south over the border before a man could even blink. Hell, he himself had done some cattle thieving back when he rode against the Red legs but... that was another story.

Sometimes it happened that way on a long drive; one man or a whole group of men would rub others on the crew the wrong way—often over the littlest thing—and nothing short of being driven off would stop the distrust and dislike that prevailed over the targeted man and his friends.

Jack suddenly resolved to keep his eyes open, but not let other's quick judgements color his own view. Con, at least, had gone out of his way to make Jack feel welcome. Just because Jack didn't much care for Con's little brother didn't automatically mean that both men were scoundrels.

He and Reb walked slowly to the remuda and found Latigo waiting patiently to take the reins. "You don't need to stay awake for me, Latigo," Jack murmured.

Whereas Latigo smiled and answered, "Taint fer you, suh. I stays awake for old Reb here."

Then, he gently pulled the bridle and bit from Reb's mouth and started rubbing the big buckskin down with an old blanket. Jack could have sworn that his horse grinned as he walked to the night hawkers' wagon for some much-needed rest.

## Chapter Twenty

Con waited for an hour and a half before he crept out of bed. According to his pocket watch it was about 3:35 in the morning, and he could hear the sporadic splatter of rain drops on the canvas overhead. Ballard's breathing was slow and steady, almost a snore and he muttered fitfully, signaling to Con the man was dreaming and his dreams weren't particularly happy.

Con quietly put his boots on and grabbed his coat and hat. Then, glancing back at Jack who had turned over and was facing away from him, he moved toward the back flap and stepped outside. It was, indeed, raining lightly and the smell of damp sage and mesquite rose like incense over the sleeping camp.

Gazing about to see if anyone was awake, it looked to him like all the fires had died down and not even a mouse was stirring. Satisfied, he walked as silently as possible away from the men scattered about on the ground like cordwood. Then, moving stealthily from bush to bush and tree to tree, he headed toward the herd. Some of the cattle were lying down, but most were standing nose to nose with their heads to the ground, the usual posture for range cattle in a rainstorm.

*Perfect!* he thought, patting the inside pocket of his coat. There were also three boxes of matches in that same hidden pocket. He knew that the trick would be to light the whole string without being seen which meant that both the firecrackers and the matches needed to be dry and that he would need to kneel down and hunch over to lite the fuse, but still be able to get up and skedaddle when the string exploded.

Con moved slowly, looking for a gap in the herd place- ment which was suitable for his actions but far enough away from Curly Buck and the camp to be invisible from prying eyes. Finally, he came to a place where four or five cows had decided to bed down. There were only a few cattle standing close by, so he figured it would be the perfect place to scoot in and set off the works without scattering the herd too much.

Con stood still and watched the periphery of the herd for any action before making his move. As he watched, a bright flash of lightning flickered in the sky above, followed by the throaty grumble of thunder. He grinned.

It seemed to him, suddenly, that nature approved of his plans and was working in concert with him to start the much-needed diversion that would keep Con and Ty in the game. Wondering, for a moment, if he should abandon the plan and just let nature take its course, he paused as another flash of lightning sizzled overhead but much farther to the north.

Deciding abruptly that the storm was not going to cooperate as much as he hoped, Con glanced around once more, saw no riders, and skulked into the herd close to the prone, sleeping cattle.

Then, he hunkered down, pulled the string of firecrackers out of his coat pocket, and wasted two matches to the now pouring rain. Glancing about, Con gritted his teeth, pulled another match out—practically on top of his jeans—and put the lit match to the end of the fuse.

He bent low, watching as the fuse caught and burned quickly—too quickly! He stood up, still in a half crouch, tossed the string of crackers at the slumbering beasts and high-tailed it back to the tree line and the sleeping camp.

———

JACK BALLARD AWOKE, gasping, from a nightmare of fire and heartbreak. He'd had these dreams since Lawrence, Kansas 1863 when Quantrill's Raiders had put an end to his boyhood fantasies of honor and retribution, and they never got any easier to bear.

Shaking in dread, he wiped the sweat from his forehead and prepared to go back to sleep but realized, suddenly, that reality had overtaken his dreams and the sounds of fear and panic were happening right outside the wagon.

He threw his blanket to the side and looked toward where Con Drago should have been sleeping, but his cot was empty, Then, Jack heard Con holler from outside the wagon, "Jack! Get up, goddamit! It's a stampede!"

Heart drumming in his chest, Jack yanked on his boots, grabbed his coat and jumped out of the wagon into a maelstrom of sound and fury. Something had spooked the cattle, and the whole herd was whipping by like a living, breathing monster into sheets of driving rain.

He turned around and saw wrecked wagons, scattered campfires, clothing, gear, pots, pans, dead animals and human bodies strewn on the ground like flotsam from a flood surge. Most of the 4700 beeves had moved past the camp by now and Jack knew that they would most likely slow down and stop on their own, once they reckoned whatever danger had spooked them was behind them.

Five horses, moving together in a bunch, flew past except for one. Reb circled back around and came to nuzzle Jack's face. The big horse trembled from forelock to tail with left-over fear and he sought comfort and guidance in Jack's warm embrace.

Jack understood that Latigo must have dropped the picket line around the remuda when he heard the stampede roaring up on the camp, and he blessed the man's courage. Deciding to go and see if the horse handler was okay, he grabbed Reb's mane and scrambled aboard.

He rode past what was left of their camp and saw that all the able cowboys were tending to the injured, and noticed lanterns being lit in the false dawn. Riding up on where the remuda had been stationed, Jack saw the big black man on the ground weeping and rocking back and forth as if his heart would break.

Jumping down, Jack ran to the man and saw Latigo holding something in his arms.

"Latigo, you okay? What you got there?" Jack murmured.

Then, looking down at what Latigo held, Jack saw the limp and battered body of Bobby Joe True. The boy's white, blood-streaked face stared up at the sky with empty eyes, and the falling rain pooled in those lifeless blue orbs and ran down his cheeks like tears. Jack knew that the kid had gone on to his reward.

Still, oh God, it hurt. Both Jack and Latigo hung their heads and wept.

## Chapter Twenty-One

Bobby Joe wasn't the only casualty. Two other cowboys, including Merrill Fairweather had fallen under the thundering hooves of the stampeding cattle and sadly the cook, Leroy Smithers had been trampled to death as well. Several cowboys were digging graves close to the tree line and Jack thought to join them in their grim task, but Tom Orr strode up and snapped, "What in tarnation just happened?"

The man was livid and trembling with anger. Jack said, "Don't rightly know, sir. I was sleeping when I heard the commotion, but Con yelled at me to wake up and when I climbed out of the wagon the beeves had pretty much gone on their way."

"So," Orr glared suspiciously, "Con was with you the whole time?"

Jack wasn't sure how to respond. He'd been asleep, after all, and couldn't exactly account for Con's every movement when he was sawing logs. Still, Tom was staring at him, seeking an answer, and Jack replied, "Like I said, sir, I was sleeping, but I think Con was with me the whole time…"

Orr studied Jack's face like he was searching for sign, and finally looked away. "Well, I got two dead men, one dead boy, four dead horses and God knows how many dead or injured beeves. Two other men are hurt bad… so bad, we need to find a good doctor."

Jack asked, "Who got hurt, Tom?"

Orr sighed. "One was Fergus O'Nally. He got stepped on and can't feel nothing below the waist. The other man is Hitch Potter."

Jack shook his head. That old bandit was pure joy to work with and he was loved by the whole crew. Fearing the worst, Jack asked Tom how bad Hitch's injuries were.

Orr replied, "Somehow, when Hitch was situating the cook wagon's tongue northward, he got kicked in the head. He's got a big goose egg and a gash on his scalp, and he won't wake up. That's got me worried enough to want a doc's help." He heaved a frustrated breath. "Okay, here's what I want to have happen and I hope you will help," he said, looking at Jack with raised eyebrows.

"Sure thing, sir, whatever you need."

Orr nodded. "Okay, Fort Griffin is close… probably no more than fifteen miles north of here. I want you and two other men—Curly Buck and young Steve Turner—to haul Hitch and Fergus to the fort. The Army has a good doctor and I'm hoping we can save our men's lives better there than out here on the trail."

Jack nodded. "Sounds good, sir. We'll get going right away." Jack turned around, looking around for Curly Buck and the tow-headed lad named Stevie T. Then, he noticed a wagon coming toward him and saw Curly sitting on the driver's bench.

Curly pulled the wagon to a stop and said, "We got both men loaded up, Tom. Besides finding a doc for Hitch and Fergie is there anything else you want us to do while we're at the fort?"

Tom shook his head. "Just wait for us. We should be there in a couple of days, if not sooner. I heard that most of the herd is settled in a about mile ahead. We need to bury our dead and clean up a bit, but we also need to make it to market before anything else happens."

Turning away with a disgusted snort, Tom Orr marched over to where his hired hands were digging graves for their fallen compadres.

———

JACK COULD SEE the high palisade walls of Fort Griffin in the distance and sighed with relief. The trip had taken far longer than he wanted, but they'd needed to go slow for the injured men in back of the wagon. They had also needed to thread their way carefully through the scattered remnants of Tom Orr's herd.

Most of the cattle were settled now and looked at the cowboys who were trying to herd them back into order with befuddled expressions as asking, what *happened to you fellers... where've* you *been?*

Curly Buck stirred in sudden alarm. "What's that, can you see it?"

Jack stared ahead and saw what appeared to be an Indian encampment on the outskirts of the big Army fort. "Looks like a small band of Indians... Comanche, maybe..." he murmured. "I know the army has been rounding up a lot of tribes around here. I see guards just outside the gates of the fort, so there must not be too many braves left—just old men, women and children."

Stevie picked his gun up when he heard Curly Buck whispering to himself and saw that he had picked up his long rifle, cradling it across his lap.

Jack said, "What are you doing, you two? I hope you're not planning on shooting one of them?" His tone was light-hearted, but Jack's nerves were tingling in alarm.

Curly said nothing but after an uncertain moment he placed his rifle back in the boot and muttered, "I won't start nothin' if they don't." Looking relieved, Stevie put his rifle down as well.

What Jack didn't know and Curly didn't volunteer was that the retired Texas ranger recognized this tribe very well. According to the signs painted on their tipis, this was the same band that had once taken Buck and his fellow rangers' prisoner and had tried their best to kill him. Curly still had the scars to show for his time spent amongst them.

The wagon moved slowly past what was left of the once fearsome tribe. Jack, Curly and Stevie T were mostly ignored by the tired and grubby men, women and children who were gathered around a small fire, butchering a dog. They were a pitiful-looking bunch and Jack couldn't help but feel sorry for their plight.

Still, he heaved a sigh of relief as the fort's walls loomed up in front of them. But then an ancient, raggedy man with an outlandish, spooky-looking head-dress hobbled toward them waving a feather-festooned stick in the air over his head. Curly leaned backwards as the oldster drew near and he fumbled frantically for his rifle.

The old man then pointed at Curly and wheezed, "That man is cursed—CURSED! He will bring no end of trouble to those he travels with and he will die, soon! Very soon!"

His words were spoken in heavily accented Spanish, which Jack understood perfectly well, but Curly shuddered. "What'd he say, Jack? What did that old medicine man just say to me?" Suddenly, Madam Fortune's whispered warning and the tearful worry in Consuela's eyes rose up in his mind.

Deciding to lie, even if it was just to get Curly to lower the rifle which was aimed dead-center on the old Indian's chest, Jack said, "It was just gobbledygook, Curly. I have no idea what he's going on about... Look, the army boys are opening the gate."

The old man was behind them now, although Jack could hear him going on and on about Curly being a cursed man. The gates were wide open and as Jack drove through the high log enclosure, he vowed that the only person who would know about what the old man had uttered would be Tom Orr.

Nodding to himself, Jack figured that Tom would know what to do with this latest intelligence. Gobbledygook or not, this sort of thing could ruin a trail drive, sure as shooting.

## Chapter Twenty-Two

FERGUS O'NALLY STARED UP AT JACK WITH SCARED EYES. He had just been told that his back was broken, and the doctor thought it unlikely he'd ever walk again. Curly had already sent a telegraph back home to Fergus's wife and children letting them know to come pick him up at the fort and take him back home.

Curly Buck had also assured them that Tom Orr would be footing the cost of transportation and any incurring medical bills, since the accident had happened on his watch. Jack was somewhat surprised that Curly had promised so much without Orr's knowledge but had no doubt the offer was valid.

"You'll be okay, son," Jack murmured to the stricken young man. "Sorry this happened to you but at least you survived to tell the tale. We lost three good men to that wreck."

Nodding as a tear escaped his eye and ran away to dampen the pillow, Fergus murmured in a heavy Scottish burr, "Aye, Mr. Ballard, I know it. Still, what am I gonna do now?"

Jack shrugged. "Don't rightly know, but just because a man loses the use of his legs don't mean he can't do a good job at living, right? Curly told me you and your people raise fine horseflesh... maybe you can sink your teeth into that. You do the pencil-work and let the rest of your kin do the handling?"

Fergus nodded. "Aye, that might work, sir. Just don't know about anything right now." Sighing, he looked away and stared bleakly at the wall to his left.

Jack touched his shoulder. "You just get some rest now, okay? I'll be back later to check on you."

Fergus gave a slight nod and closed his eyes as Jack walked away to check up on Hitch, who still hadn't opened his eyes. There were six cots in the ward and four of them were occupied; one by Fergus, one by Hitch and two more with Army's soldiers.

One soldier had been shot with an arrow while out on patrol. The arrow wound was not life threatening, but the subsequent infection surely was. Jack winced as he walked by—the young man lay in his cot, white as a sheet and close to going under from the high fever raging through his body.

For a second, Jack fancied he saw a shapeless, black shadow crouching over the boy's head but slowing to a stop, he studied the area closely and realised he must have simply been witness to a quirk of sunlight and shadow as they fought for dominance in the sick room.

The other patient sleeping between the dying boy and Hitch Potter looked terrible with his face swollen to twice its normal size, but Jack was told the kid would be alright. The young private had been bitten on the cheek by a rattler while crawling around on the ground building fence lines.

Seeing no dark shadow lurking over that boy, Jack shook his head and continued toward Hitch's cot, heaving a large leather notebook up under his right arm. He had gotten an idea, although it was probably stupid. Still, he was willing to try it if it made an impact on the old man's slumber.

It was close to evening time, and Jack had noticed over the last couple of hours that although Hitch barely stirred when the doctor waved smelling salts under his nose, slapped his cheek or hollered in his ear, Potter would turn toward human conversation like a flower toward sunlight.

For as long as Tom Orr had known Hitch, the old man had carried his large notebook with him. It was filled with stories, anecdotes, newspaper clippings, fairy tales, songs, and poems. It was a cherished, life-long diary and Hitch was closer to it than he ever would be to anyone or anything else.

So, right before he, Curly Buck and Stevie T had headed to the fort for a doctor, Tom had run up to the wagon and handed the big notebook to Jack. "Keep this safe, Jack, and give it to Hitch when he wakes up, okay? It's important to him."

Now, seeing how Hitch responded to the spoken word, Jack had decided to bring the book in to see if it might bring the old boy out of his heavy stupor. Looking down at Hitch Potter, Jack thought that, if anything, the man's heavy sleep had deepened, and Jack's heart sank. He had seen younger, stronger men succumb to less than a hoof to the noggin, and he was afraid that Hitch was going to die.

He sat down in a chair by the cot, opened the notebook and grabbed the first thing he saw—a scribbled down poem. Taking a deep breath, Jack recited,

### Cowboy's Heart

I got no family,
I got no place to go
I don't got nothing but the rodeo
To tend to my soul.
I bask in summer kisses
And feel the winter's bite
In all kinds of weather,
You'll see me test my might.
Against the doggies,
and the bulls,
the ponies, and the culls,
every animal has its place which is
More than I can say.
Cause no one loves my face.
So, its town to town I go
bucking wild horses,
Riding the rankest bull,
counting seconds on the
big money hide,
The rodeo is my final ride

Jack looked up with a blush. He had let his voice rise to make sure that Hitch heard the words, but in doing so had gotten everyone's attention. Fergus was staring over at him, and so was the snake-bit boy, Stevie T, the Army doc and even Curly Buck who had just come back from a bath.

There was a small round of applause, and then Jack heard old man Potter complain, "Of all the things you could have read to me, you just had to pick that one. That's the worst piece of crap I ever wrote, Jack!"

## Chapter Twenty-Three

APPROXIMATELY TWENTY MILES SOUTH OF WHERE HITCH was slowly gaining consciousness, Mateo was riding his horse slowly along the herd's back trail. He was looking for something—although at the moment, he knew not what. It was just a feeling that something was wrong—an instinct honed by years on the run.

He had been dozing when the stampede occurred—a light and fitful sleep troubled by thoughts of his own past and the news young Bobby Joe had shared about the Drago brothers strange, nocturnal activities. He had awoken once or twice to the flash of distant lightning, and the throaty rumble of thunder but sensed nothing out of the ordinary.

Then, he had fallen asleep again and was startled awake when he heard something new and out of the ordinary; a series of pops, like distant gunfire, or the sound of corn ears warming over hot coals. He listened closely for a repeat, but then the herd had spooked, and the rodeo was on leaving many cowboys dead, including his young friend, Bobby Joe.

Mateo's chest felt heavy with grief. He was not one to make friends easily, but Bobby was different. His wide eyes, goofy grin and earnest desire to become a cowboy, despite his fears had warmed Mateo's soul and brought him out of his self-imposed exile more than anyone else he'd met since he'd killed his step-father.

*Still,* he thought, *life goes on and the best I can do now is find out if foul-play had a hand in the boy's demise.* He looked to the churned-up ground again to see what, if anything, was there. Suddenly, he heard a shout.

"Hey, whatchu doin' there, Mexie?"

Mateo looked up and saw Con Drago regarding him from atop his horse. He did not like being called names, although being called a "Mexie" was somewhat less insulting than some of the other epithets his brother Ty had been using lately. He smiled at Con Drago and replied, "Just making sure nothing important or useful was left behind before we head out, that's all."

Con searched the ground under Mateo's feet and heaved an inner sigh of relief. He had ridden back this way for almost the same reason—although *he* was searching for left-behind evidence. The good news was that he was pretty sure he'd set the firecrackers off about a quarter mile ahead of where they now stood and try as he might, he could find no tell-tale remnants of the crackers or the fuse string in the mud.

Still, he didn't like the Mexican dogging their back trail and stated the boss' orders with a little more urgency than strictly required. "Whal, the boss wants to head out now, and asked me to fetch you back."

Tom Orr had actually told the boys to take a rest and maybe eat a little supper before they headed out in a couple of hours, but Drago figured that Mateo wouldn't know the difference if he rode up early on the boys' siesta.

Mateo studied Con's face and realized almost instantly that the man was lying... about what, he didn't know. So, he dipped his chin and said, "Si, senor. I will head back right now."

"Alrighty then, see you back in camp," Con shouted and spurred his horse to the north as Mateo watched. He reached down and grabbed his canteen, took a deep drink and tried to figure out why the older Drago brother had lied to him. Then he shrugged in resignation. Both of those Drago men were filled with hate—maybe lying all the time about everything was simply a part of their hatefulness.

Mateo brought his horse up into a trot and started back toward camp as well. But after maybe a hundred yards a hot whine filled the air by his left ear and his hat flew off his head. As cool moisture trickled down his neck and pain replaced shock, Mateo flung himself off his horse, using the animal's body as a shield from what seemed like a thousand incoming bullets.

Weapon fire rained down on where he and his black gelding stood, and the horse screamed when one of the missiles found its belly. It tried to buck the sting away but groaning, sank to its knees in the mud. Mateo went down with his horse, but knew he could find no shelter there, so he whispered his regrets to the fine gelding, grabbed his rifle from the boot and took off running in a zigzag pattern toward the tree line, bullets whizzing and whining all around him as he ran for his life.

Finally, he spied a large tree stump about six feet to his right and half skidded, half fell behind it. Gasping for breath, and heart thumping like a kettle drum, he wondered if Con and his brother had teamed up to murder him, but he shook his head in doubt.

He had watched Con ride straight ahead for at least a quarter of a mile and couldn't see how the man could have circled back around quickly enough to sabotage him here. Plus, there was too much gunfire… one man or even two-if Ty was involved in the scheme—couldn't possibly shoot that many bullets.

Heart sinking, Mateo realized that those shadowy shapes he'd glimpsed in the dusk were more than likely his faithful followers—Mexican bounty hunters, intent on selling his body-dead or alive—to the closest federales.

Fingering his ear lobe and pulling his hand down to study the blood still trickling from the wound, he knew he had been very lucky. One inch to the left and his head would have been blown off instead of his hat.

Sighing, Mateo could hear hoof beats approaching and he sent a prayer up to the blessed mother, cocked his rifle, took a deep breath and, spinning on his heels, took aim and fired.

## Chapter Twenty-Four

DAWN HAD ARRIVED IN A SHOWY DISPLAY OF PINK AND GOLD clouds. It was as pretty as a picture, but Jack stared out the window toward the south and frowned. Hitch seemed to be on the mend, and Fergus's family had arrived early last evening to whisk him away home, into an uncertain future. Curly was snoring on his cot, and young Stevie was curled up on a second cot by the door.

Jack had been told to stay put and wait for the herd to catch up with him and his compadres, but something was bugging him. He didn't know what it was, but he had the strangest feeling that something bad was happening to the herd and his new friends back on the drive.

He didn't want to disobey his boss's orders, but he was thinking about riding back. After all, Curly and Steve could sit with Hitch as the old man gained his strength— no problem, which would free him up to help Tom get the herd situated outside of the fort. Wondering if going against Tom's orders would cost him his job, Jack abruptly made up his mind.

He strode to Curly's cot and shook the man awake. "Curly, wake up," he whispered. Instantly, Buck's eyes flew open and his right hand dropped toward his gun belt. "Whoa, Curly. It's just me, Jack."

Curly stared up at him and mumbled, "What's up, Jack? Something wrong?"

Ballard shook his head. "Nah, everything's okay here. It's just that I have the feeling something might be going on with the herd, and I thought I'd head back, if you didn't mind."

Curly frowned. "What d'ya mean, something's wrong with the herd?"

Embarrassed, Jack shrugged. "Nothing I can explain, really, it's just a feeling. Still, it's strong. Do I have your permission to head on back there, in case I'm right and the boys need some help?"

Curly looked away for a moment. A part of him wanted to tell the new hire to stow his "feelings" but recently his pragmatic view on life had changed to accommodate premonitions, foresight, and supernatural mysticisms he would have scoffed at before meeting Madame Fortune and his girlfriend, Connie.

Glancing back at Jack, who stood patiently awaiting his orders, Curly thought, *who am I to ridicule a man's gut instincts? I'm as spooky as scarecrow these days!*

Nodding, Curly said, "Sure, don't see why not. Stevie and I can keep an eye on old Hitch until you and the herd get here. Besides, if all went well last night, they should only be about ten or fifteen miles out."

Jack nodded. "That's what I was thinking, too. So, I'll be heading out, and will see you later on this afternoon, okay?"

"Okay, Jack. And, take it easy... if something bad *has* happened, be real careful that you don't end up being another casualty."

Jack clapped his hat on his head, picked up his saddle bag and headed out to the Army stable to ready Reb for another ride.

———

MATEO STARED out at the rising sun and shivered. He was covered in blood, sweat and dust and he knew that his shoulder wound was starting to fester. He wondered, blearily, why his boss hadn't sent someone back to check on his missing vaquero but was too hurt and exhausted to worry over it too much. The only thing that concerned him now was how many Mexican bounty hunters were left after their sunset gunfight.... Three? Four?

Once he'd jumped from behind the stump and opened fire, Mateo was dismayed to see that there were six men riding together in the Mexican posse. He knew he'd killed two of the men he shot in the first volley. One flew backward off his horse after Mateo drilled a bullet hole in the middle of his face. Then, he'd turned slightly and fanned his right-hand pistol, shooting the second bounty man in the neck. With a spray of bright red arterial blood, the Mexican slid off his horse and landed on his head in a puff of dust.

Mateo had then spun on his heels and dove behind the stump again to reload, but one of the remaining pistoleros' bullets punched a hole in his left shoulder, effectively rendering his arm useless. Fumbling around frantically, he managed to pull his left-hand pistol from his gun belt and leaning over, he shot toward his pursuers.

He heard an anguished scream, but it issued from an equine throat, and Mateo cursed. He did not like using horses in a fight, thinking that the animals had given enough—they didn't deserve to be used as shields in human battles as well. But, knowing he had wounded the animal, he wished now that it had fallen dead. A horseless killer was almost as vulnerable as he was, and probably no match for him in an all-out gunfight.

Mateo heard hoof beats moving away and after a few moments, a loud shot. Listening carefully and hearing a heavy thud, he realized the horse he'd wounded had just been put down for good. Shaking his head, Mateo stared ahead and saw that he was on a rocky precipice. He winced as he fell to the ground and wriggled on his belly toward the edge of the outcropping.

Looking down, he saw an animal trail etched into the side of the small cliff he now perched on. Mateo stared over his shoulder and saw that the bounty hunters were still about five hundred yards away, grouped together and staring down at the dead horse at their feet.

Mateo studied the landscape carefully and thought that he could shimmy over the edge and crawl down the side of the cliff to what looked like a small cave. He realized, as well, that from the angle he was at, the cave might be nothing more than a shelf of rock. Regardless, the bounty hunters would have a tough time getting a shot off at him if he hid there through the night.

*And, if nothing else,* he glared, *they will be perfectly visible to me, if they try to sneak up on me while I'm hiding behind the rocks!*

He was wounded, in terrible pain and bleeding copiously from his shoulder but he took a deep breath and slid carefully over the edge of the rocks. He started to slide almost immediately, and his boots scraped for purchase, landing in a scruffy stand of mesquite. Heart pounding, he watched as a scorpion skittered across the dirt and gravel just inches in front of his nose before disappearing into the scrub.

Then, knowing that the pistoleros would come running as soon as they noticed he was no longer hiding behind the stump, he crept down the side of the rocky cliff face using only his right arm and hand and cursing the loose rocks and sand that made far too much noise as they dislodged and fell away to the valley below.

Finally, he made his cautious way to what was, indeed, a small cavern. Stepping onto the shelf of rock, he smelled the strong odor of ammonia, announcing that this cave was home to a host of bats… or maybe a panther. Praying that if the previous occupant was a panther it was long gone, Mateo groaned out loud and laid out flat on the ground in painful exhaustion.

He knew that he'd left a trail of blood behind him as he climbed down the cliff, but it was too late now, and he was too tired to try and hide his back trail. Seeing stars and feeling sick to his stomach, he knew that he would probably die of blood loss before the bounty hunters finally caught up with him.

# Chapter Twenty-Five

As anticipated, the herd was about ten miles away from the fort and Jack rode up to where Tom Orr sat his horse watching him approach. Frowning, Orr asked, "What's the matter, Jack? Did one of the boys die?"

Jack shook his head and gave a slight smile. "Nah, Hitch is doing great, Tom. Poor Fergie probably won't walk again, though—the Army doc said so. Still, he's safe in the bosom of his family now. Best medicine for him at this point, I'm thinking."

Tom Orr nodded in relief, but the question of Jack's presence remained in his eyes. Noticing, Jack said, "Boss, I know you told me to wait for you at the fort, but I had the craziest feeling that something... something bad was happening to you men, or to the herd. Was I wrong?"

Orr scratched his head after removing his dusty hat. "Well, as you can see, everything is okay—besides losing our cook, little Bobby Joe and two other men. About a half dozen others are injured, too, but we're coping."

Nodding, Jack asked, "How 'bout the herd, Tom? How many did we lose?"

Orr smiled, "Good news there, I guess. Looks like we lost one cow and her calf. A pity, but we'll be eatin' good the next few days."

Jack stared about at the slow-moving herd and shook his head. "And I was so sure something was wrong here. Listen, if you want to fire me or dock my pay for heading back here against your orders, I wouldn't hold it against you none…"

Orr was shaking his head. "No way, Jack. I appreciate your concern, really. Wish I had more like you on my crew. Speaking of which, I wonder if you would mind stepping into our vaquero's shoes for a while? At least until we hit Sweetwater—where I might be able to pick another hand up for the rest of the drive."

Jack raised an eyebrow. "Vaquero? What, did we lose Mateo too?"

Orr nodded. "Yup—oh, he didn't die on me, but he did take off to greener pastures, I guess. Con told me that he saw Mateo at the back of the herd and told him we were lighting out, but he never showed. This drive is so far behind schedule now, I felt we couldn't wait for him to show… besides he knows where we're headed." Looking disgusted with life in general, Tom Orr screwed his lips up and spat on the ground.

Studying his boss's face, Jack felt a prickle of alarm. Not wanting to question Tom's decision making, Jack asked, "Tom, is Mateo in the habit of taking off, or lagging behind when things go bad?"

Orr frowned and looked away to study the low mountains in the distance. He bit his lip and then said, "Unfortunately, yes, he is. He's done it twice since he hired on—once after his mother passed, and once when he thought Mexican federales were on his ass. Said, he didn't want to bring trouble down on his friends."

Jack shifted in his saddle and asked as respectfully as he could. "So, did you believe him both times and did he finally come back, as promised?"

Looking uncomfortable, Orr nodded silently. Then he said, "You know what? Now, I'm starting to wonder. Both times Mateo's left he had a damn good reason, he always asked for permission and he's always come back as quickly as possible. Plus, he's not the kind to light out at the first sign of trouble."

He glared at nothing, adding, "Now I feel terrible, but with everything going on, I've been too distracted to notice that something might have happened to a good hand ... Dammit!"

Turning to Jack, Tom said, "Jack, maybe now that you're here, you could ride back and check. If Mateo *did* ride off, that's okay—he ain't exactly hog-tied to the Triple T ranch. Still, I would hate to think we just up and left him, especially if he's in some kind of trouble."

Jack nodded, tipped his hat and said, "I'm off now. Tom, you're only about ten miles from the fort—and they're expecting your arrival. If Mateo *is* gone, he's gone, but if he's in some kind of jamb, I'll fetch him back, okay?"

Tom nodded with a tight-lipped smile and said, "Yeah, bring that young man back if you can, but if you don't see him, take care. I need you for the rest of this drive."

Jack nodded and took off at a gallop.

MATEO AWOKE WITH A SNORT. He wasn't sure what startled him awake, but the sound of loose gravel falling had disturbed his fevered dreams-again. Twice now, he'd awoken to the stealthy approach of his pursuers. He was sure one of the bounty hunters was either dead or badly injured. Mateo had shot into the darkness a few hours earlier, heard his bullet strike flesh and then listened to the man's screams as the force of the bullet catapulted him off the cliff to the valley below.

Mateo was pretty sure the man had company with him but that man (or men) had lost their nerve and fled back to the top of the cliff—until now. Mateo stared out at the sunlight with dazzled eyes and knew that it wouldn't be long before the fever that wracked his body took away any chance he might have of defending himself against these enemies.

He tried to count the men he'd killed but he was even less certain now than he'd been yesterday. Were there three men remaining, or four? Groaning, he acknowledged that he could-maybe-hold off one more man, but no more than that.

He shook his head in frustration and a tear escaped his right eye and ran down his cheek. He hated being pinned up here like a cornered skunk and felt ashamed at the way he was about to die; alone, lying in bat shit and dried bones. Still, he vowed to fight to his ignominious end and tried hard to steady the pistol that was shaking like a leaf in his hand.

Another rattle of loose gravel and suddenly, the air outside exploded with gunfire. He heard screams, returning gunshots, cries of pain and the sound of boots running across the loose scree. Mateo cocked the hammer on his pistol and prepared to meet his maker. Then, he heard an amazing thing.

"Mateo, is that you in there? Don't shoot me, por favor... it's Jack Ballard come to fetch you back to the herd."

## Chapter Twenty-Six

JACK HAD RIDDEN BACK QUITE AWAYS, FIGURING IF HE didn't see some sign soon, he'd better call it quits and head back to the herd before Orr lost patience with him altogether. He was just about to turn around when he spotted a large, dark hump lying on the ground in front of him about three-hundred yards away.

Looking right and left, scanning the perimeter for threats, Jack brought Reb up to a trot and headed for the suspicious-looking object. Riding closer he saw a horse—Mateo's lovely black gelding if he wasn't mistaken—lying in a pool of its own blood. Nerves now on high-alert, Jack hunched lower in his saddle.

It was obvious to Jack that their Mexican friend had been bushwhacked here, and that those same scoundrels could still be about, eager and willing to do the same to him. He quickly searched the ground around the dead horse and saw no 'Coup' sticks to mark an Indian's honor, which was a relief. Neither did he see Mateo's rifle, which meant that the young man might have gotten away.

Jack shook his head and wondered which way to go. Deciding to follow the horse's hoof prints to determine its direction when shot, Jack rode backward a few feet and saw that the horse *had* been heading east. Clicking his tongue, Jack moved forward slowly-ever watchful for enemy approach.

After riding about an eight of a mile; he suddenly saw a whole host of hoof prints intersecting Mateo's trail, and then spied the carcass of another horse. This horse had apparently been shot in the chest and laid down to die but had been partially butchered before its owner left. Bullet casings sparkled in the sunlight and flies swarmed around the animal's hindquarters. Jack turned his eyes and nose away from the sorry spectacle.

As Reb nickered fitfully, Jack looked to his right and spied a pool of blood by a large boulder. Riding up close, Jack saw more blood and a number of spent shell casings. Understanding that he was looking at where Mateo had made his stand, he frowned as his eyes tracked more spots and smears of blood leading to a rocky ledge.

He got down off his horse, fell to his belly and slithered to the edge of a tall cliff. Peering over the edge, he frowned as he watched three men creeping along a game trail leading to a small cave about thirty-feet away from where he lay. Seeing the mens' elaborate embroidered vests, silver Conchos and low-crowned hats, Jack assumed he was watching a band of Mexican bandits—the same bandits who had, apparently, bushwhacked Mateo.

Immediately and with no undue emotion, Jack pulled his pistol and shot the man in the lead. Without a sound, the Mexican man flew off the trail and out of sight, but his companions wasted no time defending themselves against the unforeseen attack. Kneeling low, the two bandits fired back, pocking the cliff face with bullet holes, and throwing shards of shale up in Jack's face.

The jagged shards bloodied his left cheek, but Jack fired again, putting a hole in one of the Mexicans' chest causing him to cry out in pain and fury before crumpling to the ground. The last man made a frantic leap over his companion's dead body, but Jack ended his flight with a shot to his center-mass.

Blood running steadily down his face, Jack studied the trail for more banditos, but after a few minutes saw no activity, and finally started to climb down the cliff face. Gazing at the ground below him in a small valley, he saw a number of horses, standing still and grazing the grass at their feet. Two of them had their owner's bodies draped over the Mexican saddles. One other body littered the ground and Jack wondered if Mateo had gotten off a shot at that man before he'd showed up.

Taking a deep breath and letting his heart settle down a bit from the sudden death toll, Jack studied the men he'd just shot and hoped they were dead. He would need both his hands and feet to scale the rocky cliff. He climbed down, looked at the men he'd shot, realised they were both dead and then swiftly crept toward the cave entrance. Finally, he came to a stop and called out, "Mateo, is that you in there?"

————

TOM ORR SAW JACK, Mateo and four strange horses riding slowly toward the herd. Mateo was on an unfamiliar horse and slumped over in the saddle. Spurring his mount, Orr galloped toward his cowhands and saw that Mateo's left side was coated with blood—much of it shiny and wet. The young man's face was as white as a sheet and he cursed himself as an insensitive fool.

He had been so worried about getting his cattle to market... about being the first Orr to make it rich, he'd completely forgotten that the success of his mission depended wholly on his cowboys. Staring at the young vaquero's wan face, Orr resolved then and there to be a better man going forward, instead of putting worldly riches ahead of the human men and women riding by his side who were helping make his dreams come true.

He rode up close and said, "Stop! Jack, wait here while I bring a wagon close-by, okay? Looks like our boy here was shot..." Turning around in his saddle, he whistled and shouted, "One of you men bring a wagon back here, Pronto!"

Jack nodded. "Yessir," he replied. "A pretty big crew of Mexican bandits jumped him, I'm guessing. Mateo took care of the majority of them, but I finished them off and brought our boy back to the fold."

One of the herd's wagons rattled toward them, and Orr scratched at the heavy growth of beard on his face and chin. "Banditos? Maybe... I'm more inclined to believe those were Mexican bounty hunters. Hopefully, they weren't entirely sanctioned by the Mexican government, but even if they were, we should be able to buy our way out of any reprisals."

Jack frowned. "Is Mateo a criminal, Tom? I've gotten to know him—a little bit—over the last couple of weeks and I never would have pegged him as an outlaw."

"No!" Tom exclaimed and blushed slightly. "Sorry, but

he's not what the Mexican authorities would have us believe. Mateo told me the story when he first hired-on, and it's not my place to repeat it. But what he did was for the sake of honor—and no less than I would have done, if our positions were reversed. Still, you know what can happen when money changes hands."

Indeed, Jack knew all too well what money could buy and in his own personal experience; how quickly justice could be bought and sold. He watched as Mateo was gently pulled down from his borrowed horse and placed in the back of the wagon.

Jack didn't think the bullet wound in his shoulder was fatal, but the young man was as hot as an oven and he knew that infection was the principal enemy now. Turning to his boss, Jack said, "I think that if we make him as comfortable as possible with plenty of blankets, pillows and water, we can get Mateo into the Army doctor's hands. They seem to be pretty good…"

Tom nodded emphatically. "Agreed. We'll move out right away." He started to ride off and then pulled his horse up short. Turning around, Tom said, "Thanks for saving my man, Jack. I owe you one."

Jack nodded, and answered, "Just doing my job, sir."

## Chapter Twenty-Seven

Two days later Tom Orr, Jack Ballard and Curly Buck stepped inside a low, ramshackle building on the south end of Main Street in Sweetwater—a civilian outpost about a half mile from Fort Griffin. The town was host to many business owners who catered to the needs of the Army boys stationed at the fort and home to an array of nefarious characters.

The fort's colonel had warned them to take care while visiting, as many a gunfight had erupted in the town's dusty streets and advised them that the criminal element had just as much power in Sweetwater as law-abiding citizens.

Tom, Jack and Buck had no intention of getting more involved in the town's affairs than hiring one or two hands to take the place of the cowboys and the Mexican vaquero who had fallen during the stampede. Happily, Old Hitch was on the mend and had volunteered to take Leroy Smither's place in the cook wagon.

"I'm a superior cook, boss," he'd declared from his sick

bed. "I'm as good a cook as any old French chef, and if you just give me enough time that my noggin don't ring like a bell every time I twitch a muscle, I'll prove it to ya!"

Indeed, Tom knew that Hitch had hired on as a cook for many outfits in his earlier years. He'd just grown tired of cooking and had wanted to ride with the cattle rather than put up with the same old gripes and complaints that accompanied most trail cooks' culinary efforts.

But Orr also knew that trail cooks often worked harder and put in more hours than most of the cowhands. Hitch really just wanted to work his usual ten to twelve-hour days and be free to scribble in his notebook, drink whiskey and play cards of an evening, and Tom felt that Hitch deserved to do just that after so many long, loyal years on the trail.

Frowning thoughtfully, Orr had said, "Hitch, I'll make sure you have a couple of good hands to fetch in the wood you two cooks need, and do the dishes, too, until you're healthy enough to ride with the herd again. Agreed?"

Hitch grinned, stuck his hand out to shake and said, "Agreed, Tom, and thanks."

That had been a couple of hours ago, and now Tom and his hired men had come to town for some new hires —if there were any to be found. So far, though, it looked there were no "good men" around, only ruffians and scallywags looking for a quick buck—easily and illegally attained if possible.

Tom had written out a sign that read; **Trail Hands Needed—Sign On Here**

But so far, there had been no takers. Orr frowned and mumbled, "What's wrong around here? Don't any of the men in these parts want an honest job?"

Jack shrugged, thinking, *Looks like most of these boys are as happy as clams being on the wrong side of the law... wonder who, and where, the sheriff of this town is?*

"I sure hope Mateo pulls through," Curly Buck murmured softly. He was not particularly close to the young Mexican, but he was becoming convinced that this drive was cursed. Not normally a man prone to fits of fright, Curly felt death's bony fingers plucking at him and thought of his beautiful Connie with forlorn longing in his heart—which was suddenly screaming at him to WATCH OUT!

Orr shrugged. "Army doc says Mateo's fever is coming down and that he'll probably pull through... it's just going to take time—and time is one thing we ain't got right now. Just as soon as we can find us a couple of hands, we need to light outta here. If Mateo is too sick to move, he can catch up with us later."

Buck shook his head and moaned, "Tom, I hate to repeat myself, but this drive is bad business. I can feel it in my bones!"

Orr glared, put-out, finally, with his best man's constant dire predictions of doom and gloom concerning his cattle drive. Turning to Curly, Orr snapped, "Whal, if'n you want to leave, you just go ahead and go. I don't have for time for your sniffles right now! Honestly, if I didn't know you better..."

Just then there was a scuffle on the far side of the room. Chairs were pushed back and knocked over and a couple of alarmed shouts filled the air as the patrons sought sanctuary from the fight brewing up close to the bar. The three men turned to stare at the sudden dust-up.

"You lousy skunk! You're a damn pick-pocket!"

Jack heard a younger voice shriek, "No I ain't, ya damned fool! You gotta hole in yer pocket, I swear. Ever time you put your coins in there they roll right out on the floor—and, far as I'm concerned, the floor's fair game!"

"No way is that so… boys, grab that rascal and I'll give him a thrashing he'll never forget!"

Two big, dumb-looking ruffians stepped in and grabbed the skinny, bare-footed boy with light brown hair and bright blue eyes by his arms as he twisted and howled like a wild-cat. An even bigger and uglier version of the two ruffians got up from a poker table and advanced on the youngster with a wicked gleam in his eyes.

Then, as Jack and his companions watched, the big galoot wound up and slugged the boy so hard in the stomach his blue eyes bugged out and he gagged, turning an alarming shade of purple. The men who held the boy's arms looked to the bigger man with questioning eyes and he growled, "Let me give him one more lick to remember me by and then you can let loose a-him…"

Jack, who had seen enough, started to get up from his seat to assist the youngster, but Curly Buck put a hand on his arm. "Hold up there, Jack. Here comes the law."

Jack glanced toward the bat-winged doors at the front of the bar and saw the dark shadows of three men who'd just entered from the street. Two of the shadows launched themselves at the men who held the boy and started beating on them mercilessly. The third shadow stepped closer to the man who stood stock still, arm still raised to strike the boy, who was quick-headed enough to jerk loose and scramble away from harm.

The kid started to run toward the door, but the

newcomer seized his arm and held him tight. "Whatcha doing, Carl?" the man with a tin star pinned on his vest hissed at the man with the raised fist. "Pickin' on young-uns again?" The man spoke softly but Jack could hear his whisper from clear across the room.

Carl started to sweat, and he gazed down at his two brothers who lay unconscious on the litter-strew floor. Their attackers had finished beating them to a pulp and were now calmly sipping whiskey at the bar as if nothing untoward had just happened.

"I ain't pickin' on nobody, sheriff! That stupid kid there was robbing me of all my coin, and I was jus' teachin' him a lesson, is all!"

The tall man who had a hold of the kid's arm looked down at him and asked, "Is that the truth, Levi? Were you picking Carl's pocket?"

Levi shook his head, and squealed, "No way, Sheriff! All his coin was falling through his jeans and I was just pickin' up what hit the floor! That ain't breaking the law, is it?"

Declan—Double-Deck—McGavin shook his head and grinned. "Whal, it's twisting it a bit but not breaking it, I reckon."

## Chapter Twenty-Eight

THEN, MCGAVIN TOLD HIS DEPUTIES TO TAKE CARL TO THE jailhouse for disrupting the peace, took ahold of the boy's ear and marched him over to where Jack and his companions sat watching. Staring down at Orr, McGavin said, "I want you to hire this one on before he gets hisself killed!"

Orr's mouth sagged open and he said, "Does he have anything in the way of qualifications to recommend him?"

Declan rolled his eyes. "My word is his qualification, sir. Levi has no formal training, but he works hard. He's had to since his folks were killed in an Indian attack, and he's managed to keep himself fed and clothed for the last few years. But, as you can see, he's starting to hang out with the wrong crowd and if me and my deputies don't do something soon, he'll end up dead at the hands of one of these rotten scamps."

Hearing a chorus of complaints from the crowd, one of his heavy eyebrows rose in scorn. Turning around to face the men who'd taken offence at his comment, he barked, "I didn't see a man in here raise a hand to Levi's aid! So, I'll call you a bunch of outlaw scamps if I want to, and I'll take on any man who has an issue with my appraisal!"

The customers carefully looked away from the sheriff's wrath and McGavin turned back to face Orr. "You, there... you're the catbird of that herd stationed over by the fort?" Tom nodded, and the sheriff declared,

"I'll pay you to take him off my hands..." He pulled a wad of bills out of his left pocket and waved it enticingly under Tom's nose. "I gotta admit, Levi don't know much about nuthin', but he's a game rooster, and I aim to give him a chance at life. Will you boys help me out on this?"

Tom couldn't help but stare at the cash being offered. Ever since Mateo had tangled with that batch of Mexican bounty hunters, he'd been worried about how he was going to come up with enough money to pay off any Mexican federales that might come to investigate their citizens' disappearance. He knew that the *policia* were usually "kind" enough to look the other way, if the price was right.

Sheriff McGavin was holding about a hundred dollars in his hand, and Tom reckoned that would be enough to buy Mateo's freedom. Still, he looked to Curly and then at Jack. "Well, what do you boys say?"

Curley answered, "I say we bring him, Tom. Little Billy didn't know squat either, and he was becoming a good hand before he was..." Squinting up at the kid who, frankly, looked horrified at this turn of events, he asked, "Kid, will you do what we ask you to do without a bunch of sass?"

Levi stared up at McGavin. "Sir, do I really have to leave town? I won't get into any more trouble, I promise!"

But the sheriff shook his head. "Levi, I would take you in and train you up to be a deputy, but I'm leaving for Arizona. A new sheriff is coming but I hear he's over a month out. I also heard he's a hard case, and I doubt he'll deal with you as patiently as my deputies and I have. Nope, I mean to see you in on that drive and out of my hair by tomorrow."

Knowing he was licked, Levi's shoulders sagged, and he turned his gaze to Curly Buck and said, "I'll work for ya, sir..." glancing at Tom and Jack he added, "Sirs, I mean, and I ain't a one for a bunch of sass—I promise!"

Jack grinned. Hearing mention of little Billy Joe, his heart had sunk, but he liked this boy's spunk and figured that he could be trained up as a cow hand without too much trouble. Turning to his boss, he said, "I say we go for it, Tom. We do need help, what with our injuries."

Orr nodded. "Well, Sheriff, looks like you have yourself a deal. Problem is, we need at least one more man, and the folks in here don't seem too keen on honest work. Do you or your brothers know of any more recruits?"

Declan McGavin grinned. "Oh, I have one in mind, if you care to follow me." Looking down at Levi, he paused and murmured, "Go and fetch your things, kid. Be quick about it and meet me back at the sheriff's office, okay?"

McGavin touched the kid's shoulder and said, "I want you to go and make something of yerself, you hear me? I checked on this outfit and was told it's run by good men. Like I said, I won't be around to watch yer backside anymore, and this is the best chance I can give ya to have a decent life."

Dashing an errant tear away, Levi said, "I'll miss ya, sir, but I'll try real hard to make you proud, okay?"

McGavin nodded. "Okay. Now, go fetch your stuff, and DON'T make me come lookin' for ya!"

The boy ran off and Declan said, "If you boys will follow me, I have another candidate in mind."

Orr plucked his make-shift sign off the table, the three men polished off their glasses of beer, and then they followed McGavin out the bat-winged doors and into the bright sunlight.

————

JACK, Tom and Curly followed the sheriff outside and stopped as McGavin was met by another man wearing a star. He was heavy and red-faced, heaving for air. "Declan," he gasped, "There's a pretty good dust-up down at the Spotted Pony... it's that Angus Carruthers again, fixing to shoot Buddy Williams for hornin' in on Sally's affections. What d'ya want us to do?"

McGavin looked disgusted. "Arrest all three of them and throw them in separate cells. I'll be finished here in a little while and when I get back to the office, I'm personally escorting Sally's ass to the next stage outta here!"

Turning to the cattlemen he said, "Benny, meet Tom Orr and a couple of his hired hands, Curly Buck and Jack Ballard. Orr is in charge of that big herd on the far-side of the fort. I'm sending Levi off with them and heading over to the stables to see if I can off-load Yellow Bird too."

Jack was shocked that McGavin not only knew Tom Orr's name but his and Curly's name as well. *That was some pretty thorough investigation work*, he thought silently, as he smiled at Benny and stuck his hand out to shake.

Benny Adams shook and turned back to his brother.

"You do that, Dec, and you'll break half the hearts in town! Who'll take Sally's place for the boys' affections?" He smirked.

"I don't care who they go after, just so long as that girl's heart isn't as black as coal! Sally Lloyd just loves stirring those boys up and gets all hot and bothered when they set to killing each other. I shoulda sent her packin' a long time ago!"

Jack didn't know about the legality of running folks out of town for being flirts but doubted whether McGavin cared if his actions were legal or not. He had the real sense that the sheriff's mind was made-up and so, 'bye-bye, Sally Lloyd, and too bad for you!'

Benny laughed and sprinted south, as Declan said, "Let's head down to Stone's stable. Pretty sure that's where we'll find Yellow Bird."

He commenced walking east past a number of merchant's tables loaded down with stinking, fly-ridden hides, old guns, knives and military swords, and a table of Oriental doo-dads like metal braziers, silk scarves, and pots of powdered medicines and incense.

The mingled odors of old sour blood and sandalwood made both Curly and Jack sneeze as they walked by, but Tom was too nervous to notice. He asked, "Mr. McGavin, did you say you want to send an Indian off on the drive with us? I don't know how well he'll be received..."

McGavin stopped, turned around and sighed. Staring at each of them in turn he said, "Yellow Bird ain't just any injun. He's a Comanche chief. He lost most of his people, though, and wound up all alone wanderin' around outside of town. I took him in, okay? But the folks here... well, they're hard on him. Beat the stuffin' outta him every chance they get."

Declan screwed his lips up and spat on the road. "Thing is—he's half-blind. Whoever attacked his village spared his life, but they took his right eye out and threw it as far as they could into the desert. Robbed him of his clothes and set him loose to go and find it. I heard it was the cavalry but if so, our Army boys have gone too far!" He glared toward the fort with cold blue eyes.

Continuing, he added, "It's a miracle he survived at all. I thought he'd be okay here, but as I said earlier, I'll be leaving town soon and I'm sure that as soon as my back's turned, the citizens of this town will do away with him for good. I just can't have that happen. I done enough bad in my life—don't need to add anymore to my list of sins."

Orr responded, "Well, with all due respect, Sheriff, what in blazes am I supposed to do with a blind, Indian chief?"

McGavin grinned. "Same deal… I'll pay you a hundred bucks to let him ride on the trail with you. Fact is, he ain't all the way blind, he's really good with horses, and a pretty good interpreter. He don't speak English much, but he understands it well enough. What do you say?"

Orr looked at Jack and Curly, who both thought that their outfit was getting stranger by the moment but nodded in agreement.

"Okay then," Declan smiled. "Let's go fetch the chief."

## Chapter Twenty-Nine

THE FOUR MEN WALKED DOWN MAIN STREET ABOUT A quarter of a mile and came upon a stable/corral with a small smithy attached to the back. McGavin called out, "Hey, Chester… you around?"

Jack heard a snort and the clank of metal and then a middle-aged man stepped from the smithy area into the make-shift office. He fumbled around on a cluttered desk and picked up a pair of spectacles. Perching the glasses on his nose he peered at them and said, "Howdy, Sheriff. What can I do fer ya today?"

The sheriff grinned and said, "Came to talk to the chief. Is he in?"

The smithy looked over his shoulder toward the stalls and answered, "Ayup, think so. Unless he took off without my knowing, he's back in his little tipi."

Declan asked, "How's he doin' Ches? He feelin' any better?"

The ugly, but kind-looking stable owner nodded.

"Ayup. I think so. If he ain't, well… he don't complain about it much. Not to me, anyway."

McGavin said, "Whal, we come to take him off your hands. If he'll allow it, Yellow Bird will be hitting the trail with these men here—from the Triple T cattle drive."

Chester stared down the aisle of parallel stalls and said, "Might be for the best, Sheriff. I try to keep him safe, but I gets busy sometimes and can't always stand guard, ya know?"

McGavin nodded. "I know, Ches, and I want to thank you fer yer kindness these past few weeks."

Chester smiled and answered, "Twern't nuthin, Dec. I know a good man when I sees one." With that, the stable master gave a little wave and stepped back into the smithy area. McGavin motioned his companions forward and they headed back to the furthest stall.

Even before they walked the 30-feet or so toward the back of the barn, Jack could see what looked like half a tipi rising up over the stall rails. To his surprise, he also noted the sigil painted on the front of the canvas, which was the sign of the Comanche.

There was a tiny stream of smoke coming out the top of the little tipi structure, but the front flap was tied tight. They crowded around outside the horse stall and Declan called out, "Yellow Bird… Chief! Are you in there? We'd like a word with you if you don't mind."

At first there was no reply and then Jack saw the ties coming loose from inside the canvas… the clever contraption tickled his memory, but he forgot about it as a brown, black and blue wrinkled face emerged from the opening. Curly Buck gasped and took an involuntary step back as Yellow Bird scrambled out into the light of day and stood staring up at them with a grin.

The Indian man seemed ancient as he was seamed and crooked as an old stick. He sported a bloody lip and the side of his face was scraped raw. His two waist-long pigtails were white and liberally dusted with twigs and pieces of hay, and he had not one tooth in his head. What was most notable, however, was the lurid patch over his one missing eye.

Someone had seen fit to give the old man an eye-patch, which was a kindness, but Yellow Bird had painted the black patch with garish shades of yellow and red and drawn a new eye upon it.

The eye, although amateurish, seemed to focus with great intensity on whomever beheld it, and the pupil was spoked with radiations of blue, green and purple. The get-up made the old man look like the devil come to call, and Jack could see why the simple folks in town had it out for him.

Still, the eye patch, twiggy hair and toothless grin of their new hire was the least of it. For one look and Jack knew that he had just chanced upon an old and dear friend. He had heard the name Yellow Bird earlier and thought nothing of it. After all, many white men were named John, or Tom, or Dick or Harry. Hell, many carried his own handle—Jack. Same with the Indian people— often names were repeated over and over, like the name Yellow Bird.

But this particular Yellow Bird was someone special who took Jack back to a summer fourteen years ago, during one of the most hideous and painful times in his life. He had just run away from a band of guerilla fighters and stumbled upon Yellow Bird who was carrying the dead body of his granddaughter to his people's burial grounds and had offered the man a hand.

In return, Yellow Bird had personally picked out one of their finest horses to give to Jack as a gift—the beloved horse he still rode and had named Rebel.

Yellow Bird had stared up at Declan McGavin and shrugged agreeably at the sheriff's suggestion of leaving with the Triple T boys, and then turned around to meet his new bosses when his one bright brown eye fell on Jack. To everyone's surprise, Yellow Bird bellowed, "Hoh! Jack Ballard!" and then he stepped into Ballard's warm embrace.

———

IT TOOK ABOUT ten minutes flat to dismantle the little tipi and a couple of hours later, the cowboys said goodbye and good luck to Sheriff McGavin and rode back to the herd.

Except for a few grumbled complaints against filthy injuns riding the trail cheek to jowl with good, *white* cowhands, their new hires had settled in and were coping well with their changed situations.

The worst complainers were the Drago brothers, and Jack was not surprised. Although he still liked Con's easy smile and laconic sense of humor, the younger brother, Ty, was proving to be a handful and was in jeopardy of being let go—both for his casual cruelty toward animals and worse, his antagonism toward any man who was not white.

Somehow, Tom had heard about Ty's comments toward Latigo and his hostility toward the Mexican vaquero, Mateo. Tom's temper had exploded the night before and the whole crew could hear him scream at Tyson; "One more remark outta you, son, and you'll be kicked outta this outfit... and that goes for you too, Conrad!"

Since the brothers were now on his shit list, Orr had decided to send the miscreants out together on the Nighthawking and Jack and Curly Buck were teamed up again. Jack was relieved. Although Curly seemed to have a serious case of the heebie-jeebies, he was a good rider and a keen cowhand.

Jack was glad the drive was underway. Old Hitch was healing and sat on the cook wagon's bench seat as if he'd always been there. Levi Cummings had been assigned to the cooks and seemed to be a hard worker, although he was still shocked by his sudden change of circumstance.

Yellow Bird had taken to Latigo immediately and the two men could be seen conversing regularly in some sort of soft, made-up language consisting of Spanish, Comanche and pigeon-English. Jack smiled, remembering when Yellow Bird saw Rebel for the first time in almost fourteen years and how the horse and man had recognized each other and stood nose to nose in friendship.

Jack was happy to see the old Indian again, although his presence reminded him of a time best-forgotten—a history of blood and violence in his earlier years that he'd never quite gotten over. Yellow Bird seemed to sense this, and except for the occasional friendly wave, kept to himself, Latigo and the creatures he valued above all others—horses.

Mateo was also on the mend and had taken great pains

to thank Jack for his help against the Mexican bounty hunters. "You saved my life, mi amigo, and Mateo does not forget this. Anytime you need help, you can count on me-si!"

Jack assured the vaquero that he didn't need any help but knowing how important honor was to the Mexican people he nodded solenmly, and said, "I appreciate that, Mateo. If trouble *does* come, I'll know just who to call."

Jack grinned, seeing the relief on Mateo's face and then he saw Curly approaching on his horse. Knowing it was time to head-out, he lightly touched his rowels to Reb's sides and met the cowboy halfway to start their shift.

## Chapter Thirty

TWO DAYS HAD PASSED SINCE THE DRIVE LEFT FORT GRIFFIN and headed north. They were making good time, but Jack was weary. After a long night riding the herds back-trail, Jack had settled in for a good nap, but he tossed and turned on his bunk, caught up in a wash of memories that had not haunted his dreams in years…

*21-YEAR OLD JACK BALLARD rode the supply wagon through blazing waves of heat which bellowed up from the sere landscape like gusts from a cookstove. He took his hat off and wiped sweat from his brow with a sigh. His commanding officer had ordered him to go to Maggie Drummond's house to pick up supplies; hard tack, grease, ten sides of bacon, three boxes of fresh cream butter, two wheels of cheese, six dozen eggs, two bags of cornmeal and four large barrels of water.*

*The widow was a sympathizer to the 'Bushwhackers' cause, and when she was able, she donated to the rag-tag group of guerilla fighters scattered here and there throughout the Kansas wilds. He was now just outside the city of Lawrence, close to his girlfriend's farm. Looking back over his shoulder at the fresh goods, Jack grimaced and wondered if the butter would melt like beeswax before he got back to camp. He could see that the cheese was sweating almost as fiercely as he was.*

*Jack was a fairly new recruit to the rebel cause, but he was proud as punch to support his friends against the Northern aggressors. Ever since the blue bellies had killed his own family for being anti-slavery advocates, he'd burned to do his part in the Civil War. He had yet to be called up to the regular Confederate Army, though, and wanted to help out before the war ended entirely.*

*Jack felt that no man, or group of men—state or group of states had the right to come from out of nowhere and seize what was rightfully his. His own people had migrated to Missouri from Scotland and had worked their land for two generations! Who gave the northerners the right to grab everything his family and friends had worked for so long?*

*As for "slavery", why—Jack had seen with his own eyes that many Union troops treated the negros around them worse than their owners would ever think of doing. He, himself, didn't feel it right that one man should own another but so far, he hadn't heard any persuasive arguments on how to actually free the slaves without those poor people coming to great harm and insecurity.*

*Mainly, he'd seen too much meanness in his young life-what with the war and all, to be able to reconcile why the Northern states thought they had the God-given right to take what was his, so he'd signed up to join Quantrill's Raiders. He'd never seen the man, who was doing his best to uproot Union soldiers from the Missouri area, but he worked with one of Quantrill's trusted lieutenants in the "Blue Sash" outfit here in Kansas.*

*He was pretty green and had yet to kill a man. Also, he did more 'mule' work than anything else but still, he felt like he was doing his part to combat the Yankees. But, days like this tested his mettle. It was so hot! He recalled his pa's coon hounds who shimmied under the porch boards and laid out flat on the dark, cool earth to escape the sun's rays, wishing he could do the same now.*

*Realizing that the old mare pulling the wagon had come to a dead stop, he roused from his daydreams and clicked his teeth, shaking the reins, but the horse shivered, looked to her left and nickered with her ears laid flat on her head. Looking to his left, Jack saw a great dark cloud looming on the horizon over the town of Lawrence.*

*At the same moment, he tasted ashes on his tongue and spat out a glob of black. His blood ran cold, and he snapped the long reins over the mare's back side. "Hyah!" he shouted, and the horse bolted forward through the low brush.*

*As he and the mare made their hasty way toward camp, Jack wondered what the hell was happening in town... and possibly, his girlfriend's family farm? Nothing was supposed to happen here, and although he was new to the group of men he'd signed up with, he believed he'd have heard if Lawrence was to be a target!*

*Still—he glanced to his left again and saw lofty tongues of flame licking at the skyline. That was Lawrence alright, and it was awash in flame! Panicking now, Jack snapped the reins once more and finally flew up on his base of operations in a great gust of flying dust.*

*Jumping off the wagon he made for the center of camp where the officers usually congregated. Coming closer, Jack saw a group of strangers, and then his eyes fell on the man, himself... Quantrill. Handsome of visage, and youthful, he stood tall and* laughed as his eyes raked the blood-red sky over Lawrence. "That'll teach 'em to hurt our women and children!" he snarled with a sinister chuckle.

Jack had heard about what happened. A couple of weeks earlier, the citizens in Lawrence, tired of being victimized by Quantrill's outriders had sent men out to seize some of the 'Bushwhacker's" wives, girlfriends and small children. They had planned on using the outlaws' females as hostages to hopefully, bring their antics to an end, but there had been a tragic accident.

The jailhouse—maybe due to over-crowding or to structural collapse from a sudden squall that had soaked the area earlier, had fallen in with the women and children still trapped inside its walls. It was a horrible thing, truly a disaster, but it was an **accident**. At least, that was what Jack had heard. But now? If the man was to be believed, Quantrill and his men had just fired the town in retaliation!

Heart quaking in fear, Jack backed away and ran swiftly to his horse—an old sorrel named Squirrel. Moving quietly, he rode away from camp and then hunched low over the horse's neck and rode hell-bent for leather to where his girlfriend's family's small but prosperous farm nestled along a creek just north of Lawrence.

He got to within a half a mile of Ellie's home and knew, with sudden dreadful certainty that all was lost. By now, both he and his horse were covered head to tail in sweat, soot and ash and Jack's heart broke as he crested a rise behind his house and saw that everything—the house, the barn, loafing shed, the corral and the pig's pen was burned to the ground.

He saw a pile of burnt bodies in the front yard close to the house and getting off his horse, Jack recognized his pretty girl-friend, her parents, her Auntie Jen, her older sister, Marybeth, and her little brother, Johnny. Studying their dead bodies, he noted that each of them had been shot between the eyes before being cast onto the burning pyre her home had become.

The young man's heart turned to stone as he realized the same group of men he'd joined in with to fight the Northern troops had just visited the fires of hell on an innocent family—for no good reason but a skewed and misbegotten sense of justice!

Knowing he had nothing to lose—not anymore since his parent's death in Missouri and now the passing of his girlfriend and her whole family—he climbed back on his horse and rode south—away from Lawrence, Kansas and what would turn out to be 180 dead citizens, toward the Texas territory, where he could start anew and, hopefully, sign up with the regular Confederate Army.

He had ridden as fast and far as he could without bringing harm to Old Squirrely for about four days and was now in Texas. He didn't know why, but some deep, dark instinct was urging him to put as much distance as possible between himself and those Blue Sash boys in Kansas.

He didn't know why he should fear them now—he hadn't done anything to them and would never speak to anyone about what they'd done. His own dreadful complicity wouldn't let him. Still... he knew just how much **loyalty** meant to those men—and his sneakin' off without a by-your-leave would not sit well with them.

He was riding through a cactus dotted canyon, thinking about his girlfriend's ruddy freckles and her little brother's shy adoration, tears running steadily as rain down his cheeks when he almost ran over an Indian man who was carrying the body of a young woman in his arms. The man looked to be in his mid-forties and although his arms trembled with fatigue, he sang a song in a clear voice... an Indian tune that swelled and soared with power and grief.

Pulling to a stop, Jack looked down and said, "Hey, can I help any?"

At first the older man didn't seem to hear him, but then he quieted and looked up at where Jack sat staring down at him and his granddaughter.

"I... I need to take my granddaughter to the burial grounds... it is far—maybe twenty miles, but it must be done," he rasped.

Jack nodded. "Well, don't think my horse will carry all three of us, but if you like, I can carry your burden while you walk alongside... would that work for ya?"

The chief stared up at Jack and saw the tears that had carved rivulets down his face and the shadows of sorrow riding on his narrow shoulders. This young man, too, had suffered from some great loss and looking closer, he saw no hatred in Jack's eyes, just pity and a desire to help.

Yellow Bird nodded slowly and said, "Yes, that will work for me. Thank you."

## Chapter Thirty-One

JACK AWOKE WITH A GASP, FEELING LIKE THOSE LONG-AGO flames which had burned his girlfriend and her family to ash were just as hot now and trying to consume him where he lay drenched in sweat on his cot.

Sitting bolt-upright, Jack gazed about at the familiar wagon he and Curly Buck shared and realized the sun's heat had brought the temperature up to scorching, and with a heave he pulled himself out of his bed and opened the flap to let some air in.

Breathing deeply, he saw that they were moving up a long, gradual hill. The cattle were thirsty and moaned miserably as they meandered slowly along the incline. The cowboys looked every bit as miserable and their horses coats were drenched in dust and rivulets of sweat.

Suddenly, a tiny freshet of cool, humid air ruffled the hair plastered to his neck and forehead. Jack knew then that the herd was finally coming to the Brazos River. He grinned, thinking, *we made it to water and greener pastures, thank the Lord.*

The cattle perked up as they smelled the sultry air and the horses pricked their ears and stretched their long necks forward to sniff the sub-tropical moisture. Jack nodded and then frowned. This was good news, but also bad news.

The good news: the livestock and men could cool off and replenish their almost empty water barrels. In addition, prairie grass was plentiful here which would give Orr's herd a chance to come back up to weight before they hit the market.

The bad news: Uncertain, but Jack knew that Tom and his crew were not the only citizens looking for water and sweet grass in this part of the state. Since this was one of the most uncivilized areas of Texas, many wild Indians still frequented the swamps and wetlands surrounding the Brazos' shores.

Also, Curly Buck was growing more frightened by the day and seemed to harbor an almost superstitious dread of crossing the big river. The last three days around the nightly campfire, he'd gone on and on about how hazardous the crossing could be and how savage the Indians in this lonely Texas wasteland were.

The men were sick to death of hearing him moan, and last night Hitch had looked up at Curly with tired eyes and said, "Curly Buck, I think you should turn back around right now and head fer home. Jack Ballard can take your place, no problemo. Cuz, I tell ya, you and yer bitchin is cursin' this outfit with discontent!"

Murmurs of agreement filled the air, and Curly had stalked off alone, into the darkness.

Orr, who cared for Curly, had finally lost all patience

with his second and after Curly left, he'd turned toward Jack and publicly asked. "How 'bout it, Jack. You want to be my second?"

Embarrassed, Ballard had replied, "Nah, just give Buck a chance, okay? We'll be crossing the river soon enough and maybe then he'll settle down. You'll see."

Tom bowed his head. He too felt bad about his loyal employee and was sorry he'd opened his fat mouth in front of all the other cowhands. He wanted to grab his hasty words and shove them right back down his throat, but it was too late now.

Disgusted with himself, Tom stood up, and declared, "Time to hit the hay, boys. We won't cross the river until day after tomorrow but there's still a ways to go yet and we should be rested up for the crossing."

And now, they were here! Jack jumped off the tailgate and stretched. Curly Buck looked around from the wagon's bench, pulled the mules to a stop and said, "Boss says there'll be no Night Hawking tonight, but he is posting a few more guards, cause of injuns. I heard the cavalry's got the Comanche riled up as well as the Arapaho. I hoped to get some shut eye now, cuz I'll be sleeping with one eye open come nightfall."

Curly didn't scemed quite as 'wall-eyed' as he'd been, and Jack knew his caution was warranted. Angry Indians were always keen on bloody justice, especially when their women and children were starving to death. A whole herd of meat on the hoof would be a great temptation to any self-respecting brave and Orr's cowboys need to stay vigilant.

"You jump in back and get some sleep, Curly. I'll take

over driving. At least *you'll* catch a cool breeze. I about roasted to death in there!"

Curly grinned and disappeared into the covered-wagon as Jack climbed up onto the bench and snapped the reins. Within minutes, he heard Curly snoring gustily and grinned.

Looking forward, he saw that the cowboys were trying hard to keep the cattle from bolting, the smell of water was so keen and then he saw the blue twinkle of the river through some distant trees.

Orr shouted something, and suddenly the cowboys peeled off and let the cattle make their way toward the water. In a hasty but rather orderly rush the cattle bounded toward the shoreline and descended onto the water.

Jack took his time, although his mules and even Reb were trembling with excitement. In good time they made their way to the big river, and he unhitched the animals from the wagon. The mules and horses drank their fill, as Jack watched a herd of black-tailed deer lift their velvety muzzles, sniff their arrival from the opposite side of the river, and bound away out of sight.

———

THE DRAGO BROTHERS watched as Jack Ballard removed his shirt, dunked his Stetson in the river and poured cool water over his head and upper chest. The man grinned and shook all over like a big red dog. Con saw Jack's splendid physique, and dark auburn hair. He growled under his breath, "Traitorous bastard!"

The skinny young pup who had turned tail and ran

fourteen years ago in Kansas had turned into a fine, strapping man and Con wondered how Jack could sleep at night… and whether or not he suspected his old gang was gunnin' for him.

Con and Ty had been members of Quantrill's Raiders and then the Regulators. They had carried out their vengeance against the Northern Aggressors with pride, dignity and deadly efficiency. Sure, maybe burning out so many citizens in Lawrence that day was over-kill, but it was in retribution, not malice and was by and large a mistake.

Still, after that fateful day the Raiders were viewed by one and all as outlaws, rather than Southern sympathizers. They were forced to disperse, and many of their best and strongest members were killed outright or were forced to ground and true devilry, including Con and his little brother.

With a pang of regret, Conrad remembered those good old days when the Youngers, the James boys and even William Bonney rode with the Regulators. They were stuff of legends now and mostly either rounded up and carted off to jail, active outlaws, or dead and buried.

Con had no way of determining, even now, whether the ex-Raiders had come to a natural, organic end or if Jack Ballard had turned evidence against them, hastening their demise. Either way, though, it didn't matter. The boy had fled and betrayed his sworn oath to the Blue Sash Society—which was a living, breathing remnant of the old order of Masons-The Palm Tree Society.

Con and Ty wanted to eek out as much money as possible before they meted justice out to the traitor Jack

Ballard. But, one way or the other, Ballard was a dead man walking.

Trembling with rage, Con spat in Jack's direction and then rode off a ways to let his horse drink. Ty followed suit, grinning.

## Chapter Thirty-Two

AFTER CAREFUL CONSIDERATION, TOM ORR DECIDED TO linger for a few more days and let his stock partake of the water and plentiful prairie grass. True, his schedule was behind by about a week due to the stampede and subsequent injuries to his men, but sometimes discretion really was the better part of valor, especially when it came to money on the hoof.

The first day was tense as Orr and his men feared an Indian attack, but things were quiet, and on the second day the men relaxed, welcoming the unanticipated vacation. They took time to sleep, play cards, do a little newspaper reading, take baths in the cold water, launder their clothes and trim their beards and mustaches.

Talk around the campfire that evening was about the thorough trouncing Custer and his 7th had received the month before in the Montana Territory. The one thing veterans like Jack and Curly were used to was how fiercely independent most Indian tribes were... from one another and from other tribes within their region.

Jack had always thought that if the natives could just band together, for once, the white man wouldn't even be capable of crossing the Continental Divide. The unthinkable had clearly happened, however, to Brevet General Custer and the troops who'd traveled with him, so many of whom suffered and perished as a result of the natives' unaccustomed solidarity.

The other topic of conversation was news that GOLD had been found in the Black Hill Mountains and lots of it. Many of the younger, spryer cowboys on the drive were making tentative plans to collect their wages in Dodge City once the drive was done, and then catch a train to Idaho to try their hands at the geological bounty. Even Jack gave some consideration to this notion but wasn't sure how much he relished the idea of standing thigh deep in icy water with a pick—ax and a shovel sorting rocks from gold for the next few years.

The mood was festive and even Curly Buck, knowing his dreaded river crossing would be delayed for a while, leapt into the river and commenced to splashing the other cowhands with torrents of water.

Jack grinned as the men frolicked like children, and sat back against a large boulder, treating himself to the rare stogie. Dinner was over by now and he could smell coffee brewing in the two cook wagons. Orr was letting his guard down, but he was no fool either. This was a "dry" camp, at least until they made their way to more a populated region.

He heard soft footfalls and looked up to see Yellow Bird staring down at him with a shy smile. He held a deck of cards in his left hand and lifted his eyebrows in invitation. "Play some poker?" the old man asked, and Jack nodded with a grin.

Yellow Bird sat down, crossed his legs and proceeded to win every hand for over an hour until Jack threw his hands in the air in disgust. "One of these days, I'm gonna figure out how you do that, I swear!" he complained, and the old Indian cackled with glee.

Many years ago, Jack had stayed about two weeks with Yellow Bird's small band of Commanche Indians— mostly old men, squaws and a few children. Most of the braves had ridden off a long time ago and never returned to their home fires. He'd been treated courteously, as befitting the youngster who had helped their chief return home with his beloved granddaughter after being attacked by a roving band of Arapaho braves on the war path.

Jack had learned a smattering of their language and eaten their tart but tasty fare. But mainly, the Indians had somehow managed to grab almost every penny in his pocket besting him at poker. He dared not accuse them of being cheats and in the end, most of his money was returned to him with a chuckle and a sneer, along with a magnificent gelding, a buffalo hide, two kettles, and a fine horse blanket.

He had decided, then and there, not to gamble with an Indian again—ever.

Growing serious, Yellow Bird said, "You white men— you see the cards, but you do not listen to them! We injuns—we hear the cards speak to us and they tell us what to do."

Jack rolled his eyes but remained respectfully silent. This wasn't the first time he'd been beaten at gambling by his old friend and God willing, it would not be his last. He picked the cards up once more to deal himself another beating, when the sound of clacking spoons and a song filled the air. It was Hitch, who rarely sang, but must have felt the urge.

Jack heard a smattering of applause and watched as several of the youngsters climbed to their feet. Then, he smiled as Hitch's raspy baritone rose into the dusk.

*As I was a-gwine down the road, With a tired team and a heavy load, I crack'd my whip and the leader sprung, I says day-day to the wagon tongue. Turkey in the straw, turkey in the hay, Roll 'em up and twist 'em up a high tuckahaw And twist 'em up a tune called Turkey in the Straw. Went out to milk, and I didn't know how, I milked the goat instead of the cow. A monkey sittin' on a pile of straw, A-winkin' at his mother-in-law. Turkey in the straw, turkey in the hay, Roll 'em up and twist 'em up a high tuckahaw And twist 'em up a tune called Turkey in the Straw. Met Mr. Catfish comin' downstream. Says Mr. Catfish, "What does you mean?" Caught Mr. Catfish by the snout, And turned Mr. Catfish wrong side out. Turkey in the straw, turkey in the hay, Roll 'em up and twist 'em up a high tuckahaw And twist 'em up a tune called Turkey in the Straw. Came to a river and I couldn't get across, Paid five dollars for a blind old hoss; Wouldn't go ahead, nor he wouldn't stand still, So he went up and down like an old saw mill. Turkey in the straw, turkey in the hay, Roll 'em up and twist 'em up a high tuckahaw And twist 'em up a tune called Turkey in the Straw. As I came down the new cut road, Met Mr. Bullfrog, met Miss Toad And every time Miss Toad would sing, Old Bullfrog cut a pigeon wing. Turkey in the straw, turkey in the hay, Roll 'em up and twist 'em up a high tuckahaw And twist 'em up a tune called Turkey in the Straw. Oh I jumped in the seat and I gave*

*a little yell The horses ran away, broke the wagon all to hell*
*Sugar in the gourd and honey in the horn I never been so happy*
*since the day I was born. Turkey in the straw, turkey in the hay,*
*Roll 'em up and twist 'em up a high tuckahaw And twist 'em up*
*a tune called Turkey in the Straw.*

By now, almost every man in the outfit was on his feet kicking his heels up and many of the young'uns had locked elbows and were dancing a jig to the raucous ditty.

Looking up, Jack saw that Yellow Bird had also risen to his feet and was shuffling slowly in the Indian way, pounding his heels onto the ground and swaying to the beat.

Jack Ballard grinned and thought, *Sometimes, when you least expect it, life deals you a grand hand!* He sat back against the boulder again and smoked the last of his cigar as the song ended and evening settled in.

———

JACK WASN'T the only man who had stopped to listen to Hitch's song. A small band of Comanche fighting braves had been hiding up a hill about 500-yards away from where the white men malingered by the river. They had already stolen about thirty cattle which were even now being driven south by some of the younger members of their war party.

Technically, their mission to the river was a resounding success. The cattle they'd just stolen would keep their women, children and grandparents fed for many moons. But being rounded up and forced to move to mandated reservations by the white men had stirred the embers of their resentment which were barely banked to begin with. And now, their successful sneak attack on the herd had stirred their fury into a red-hot blaze.

The braves had decided to make war on the men as well as steal their beef. They chose to wait until the sun dipped below the horizon before attacking but just as they were about to commence, a strange clatter (which were Hitch's spoons) filled the air, and then they paused and listened as Turkey in the Straw was sung by many a willing throat.

The Indians listened, looked at one another and changed their minds. Although he did not understand a word of the cheerful ditty, their leader, a fierce man in his early thirties, found himself thinking—any group of people who could raise such a fine song up to the Gods did not deserve to die, at least not by his own hands.

As one, the braves fell back and disappeared into the darkness.

## Chapter Thirty-Three

SALLY LLOYD WAS MAD AS A WET HEN AND SHE UNFURLED
her pretty pink parasol with an irritated snap. *That nasty
old sheriff back in Sweetwater had no right!* she thought. *No
right at all to send me out on a rail like he did just because a
couple of buckaroos got into a fist-i-cuffs over my honor!*

She lifted her arm, wiped big drops of greasy sweat
from her brow and dabbed between her breasts with a
large white hanky. "Shoo—it's hot!" she muttered and
wished that a stagecoach or a wagon would show up soon
to save her from too long of a walk.

Peering ahead, she saw big cumulous clouds gathering
together on the horizon like a flock of black sheep and
she felt a warm raindrop hit the top of her head. *Dangit!*
She complained, *Looks like I'll be getting soaked before I can
catch a ride!*

After they'd left Sweetwater, she had quizzed the
coach driver repeatedly about how often coaches came
this way on any given day and he'd scratched his grizzled
old head and answered, "Pretty near two or three times a

day, Miss. As long as the fort stays open and Sweetwater's a 'boomin' there'll be plenty of stagecoaches on this road."

So, feeling the loss of her misbegotten fortune, she'd decided to jump out of the stage and make her way back to old Hide Town. *What the sheriff don't know won't hurt him,* she reasoned, *and I'll be long gone if the driver tattles on me. Why, I'll just sneak into town, grab my loot and hang low until the next stage leaves town. I'd rather not risk it but damn! I spent too much time gathering my nest egg together to let Double-Deck cheat me out of it.*

At the very back of the player piano in the parlor of the Pink Palace, sat a velveteen draw-string bag filled to over-flowing with gold, silver, jewelry and cash-notes. She'd been gathering that small fortune up since she was fifteen-years-old and she figured now was the time to grab it and set up new someplace swell like... Dodge City, maybe. She's been hearing good things about that cow town lately. Lots of money on the hoof there, which meant a lot of suddenly rich cowboys with nothing better to do than spend their hard-earned cash on her!

She wished fervently that she'd had half a chance to grab her little bag before she was stuffed, kicking and screaming, into the stage but she couldn't very well ask for help from her fellow prostitutes since a lot of her bootie consisted of stolen tips and easily recognizable rings and necklaces.

Still, she sighed in disgust, if a coach would just happen along before she melted to death, that would suit her fine! Sally glared back at the road behind her, looking for a tell-tale plume of dust but except for shimmering waves of heat, she saw nothing behind her for miles. Sighing, she set to walking again and hoped her little canteen of water would be enough to stave off serious thirst before a southbound stagecoach showed up.

Suddenly she saw some sort of mirage on the road in front of her. Coming to a stop, she shaded her eyes and stared as a number of wavy, colorful shapes broke apart and blended together again in an odd dream-like display. It was such a strange, unexpected vision she found herself smiling at her fanciful imaginings.

Then she heard a bird's cry. Looking up, Sally searched the sky but saw no birds circling even as the air filled with more raucous screeching. Confused, and suddenly afraid, Sally grabbed ahold of her satchel and turned around to flee from the approaching shapes, but then they were all around her; Indians in full battle-dress, their faces, chests, arms and hands painted red, yellow and black, their ponies painted to match.

Sally screamed as they moved in around her and wailed when she was plucked up off the ground by her hair, hit over the head with something heavy and sharp and knew nothing more—ever again.

———

TWO FULL DAYS HAD PASSED, and Tom Orr was ready to move on. He was dismayed to find out that almost 35 cattle had disappeared overnight, and his scouts had found numerous coup sticks marking the ground toward the back of the herd. It was as if the people who'd swiped his cows were daring him and his to do something about it—at their own peril.

Looking to Curly, Tom asked, "Do you recognize this sigil?"

Curly Buck nodded. "Yessir, that's Comanche, if I'm not mistaken. I reckon we're lucky to still be wearing our scalps."

Jack nodded in agreement. "Yes, the Indians are stirred up by the local cavalry, and by what transpired up in Montana last month. I'm with Curly— we lucked out that they didn't attack."

Feeling a definite tingle under his own scalp, Tom asked, "Jack, do you think old Yellow Bird has something to do with this welcome party?"

Jack shook his head. "Nah, I doubt it. Back when I first met him, he was chief to only a few oldsters, women and small children. Their braves were all killed or had abandoned years before that."

Tom nodded and then said, "Okay then. We're heading out in about two hours. I want everybody fed and watered, and buttoned up tight. This is a shallow crossing but it's wide with some fairly steep drop-offs into deeper water."

He took his hat off and swiped sweat from his brow. Then he studied the wagons which were lined up along the sandy banks. "I want the wagons to go first—and then the cattle. Most times, the head cows will watch a wagon cross water and if there's no problem, she'll decide it's okay for her brood to pass. Cows ain't known fer their smarts, but most of them trust the evidence of their own eyes... hopefully, an easy passage for the wagons will make for a smooth river crossing."

It took a couple of hours but finally, the five wagons were lined up on the south bank of the river. The cattle had been shooed away from the banks and beaches and now stood poised and anxious, as if waiting for the wagons to make the first move.

Jack shook his head and grinned. He had found Tom Orr to be both a good and bad boss. He was easily distracted and when push came to shove, his loyalties could be divided pretty easily. But all in all, he seemed to be a decent man and his instincts concerning cattle were uncanny.

He watched as the five wagons entered the river and saw three old boss cows watching them with keen, intelligent eyes. As soon as the wagons gained dry sand on the opposite side of the river, the cows bellowed and ran into the water. Sure-enough, the rest of the herd crowded in behind them and suddenly the river was filled with wet, squirming brown, black and white cowhides.

It took a while for the herd to cross. Even after their many losses, there were still over thirty-two hundred cattle in the Triple T drive, but after about forty-five minutes, they were coming to the end of the river crossing. Jack was drenched and so were the other cowboys, but it was a pleasurable feeling. It had grown hot and humid and the air felt like the inside of a Chinese bathhouse.

Suddenly, with a clap of thunder so loud it sounded like cannon fire, a streak of lightning stretched long forked fingers over the landscape and the skies opened up. Jack's horse trembled, and he reached down to comfort Rebel, saying, "Hold up there, son. You know what lightning is, remember? It'll move on soon enough."

Then, as he and four other drovers, including Curly Buck, the Drago brothers and a youngster named Petey crossed the suddenly rushing waters, a strange and horri-fying thing floated downstream toward them.

Jack's gelding was a steady hand but even his nerves fled as several rattlesnakes, deadly fangs clamped like vises around the body of a naked, drowned woman bobbed on the turbulent waves. She had long blonde hair that floated like golden gauze about the head of a battle-ax which was sunk into her skull. A third snake's jaws were latched onto her left leg and the whole bloody, seething mess rolled over and over amongst the horses, men and cattle.

It was a macabre, almost sexually brazen tableau so terrifying Jack knew he would never forget it, especially since the woman's blue eyes were fixed and staring at those who watched her with cold and bitter defiance.

Curly Buck, who had slept with Sally Lloyd a number of times over the years, remembered Connie's whispered warning, and screamed even as another mighty bolt of lightning etched the land around them in white fire.

## Chapter Thirty-Four

IT ONLY TOOK A SECOND FOR JACK TO REALIZE THAT A tornado had cooked up out of nowhere and now had them pinned in the river. Although he'd seen several twisters throughout his life, this was the first he'd actually seen in Texas. The timing couldn't be worse, and he knew that these next few moments could very well be his last on Earth.

He sighed and then gritted his teeth. *No, dangit. I ain't goin' out that easy!*

In an instant the water rose from just under the horse's bellies to over-top their heads and screaming, both horses and cattle were lifted off their feet. Some of them, like Rebel, kept their heads and started swimming toward the shoreline but some of the beasts were simply carried off down river. As Jack spurred his mount up onto dry land, he was horrified to see many beasts, and more than a few men slide under the waves and stay under—apparently drowned.

Looking back over his shoulder toward the main bulk of the herd, Jack saw a gigantic column of dust, sand, grass, rocks, bushes and gear rising in a funnel of wind, fifty-feet into the air. Even as he stared, mesmerized, he thought he heard a shrill bleat of fear and saw a black and white calf rise up into the sky above. Shaking his head in awe, Jack searched the ground and saw nothing but frantic darting shadows encased within a thick haze of dust. He could only hope and pray that his fellow cowboys would survive.

Hearing a panicked shout, Jack turned back to the water and saw Curly Buck falling or being pulled off his horse. Looking closer, he realized that a steer had come up under Buck's horse and was goring it to death. He saw blood pouring from the animal's punctured belly and grabbed his rope to try and save his friend.

Fortunately, Con had already let a coiled loop fly and Jack saw Curly, now covered by a thick coat of blood, grab the rope. But then, both the steer and the horse it had pierced did a belly-roll taking Buck down into the roiling water with them.

With a hoarse shout, Jack laid his rowels against Rebel's side and they took off at a quick trot down the shoreline, but rubble was everywhere—both old and new. He was searching the water, praying that Curly had disentangled himself and gotten clear of his dying horse, but Rebel stopped with a startled snort as a low hum filled the air. Suddenly, even as Jack felt his cheek heat up in agony, Rebel was bucking rodeo and Jack was flung from the saddle.

Apparently, one of the logs had either blown down in

the tornado's winds or rolled over exposing a wasp nest the size of a half-bale of hay. Wasps swarmed the air and both Jack, and his mount felt their wrath. The angry buzzing seemed to go on forever but finally, the wind swept them away leaving Jack and Rebel covered in painful, throbbing stings.

Jack climbed to his feet and stared toward the water again but Curly Buck, his horse and the steer were long gone—swept away by the storm's swell. Sighing in grief and discomfort, he felt around in his saddlebag for his medicinal ointment. Placing a dab on the stings that graced both of his cheeks, his neck, and the back of his left hand, Jack commenced to doctoring his poor horse. Rebel had suffered the most, Jack found, as he smeared the paste over fifteen stings on the horse's neck, belly and hindquarters as the animal shook with pain and nerves.

The twisters main fury was tapering off now and swallowing his sorrow, Ballard scanned the slowly settling waves. He saw a youngster named Willie bobbing up and down on the water and calling for assistance. "Help!" he cried, "I cain't swim!"

But the boy was riding a broken tree limb and even as Jack watched, the branch sailed onto shore. Willie jumped off and then ran onto higher ground as fast as his feet could carry him. Most of the crew had turned around and was headed back to the river and Jack saw that the herd was long gone, spooked up by the twister and determined to flee the storm's wrath.

The horrible, high-pitched sound the tempest made in its passing was gone as well, and Jack thanked God for that small blessing. He'd heard tornados before but always from a certain distance. This one was simply too close, almost on top of him, and he remembered thinking that the wind sounded like the angel Gabriel's horn; an earth-shattering, ringing peal unsuitable for human ears.

Tom Orr trotted up on his winded horse. He was drenched with water, sweat and fury. He looked Jack up and down and studied the carnage on the beach for a second. Then, he asked, "What happened to your face?"

Jack shrugged, "Ran smack dab into a wasp's nest. They got me and my horse pretty good." Jack could feel his cheek swelling up as he spoke.

"Sorry about that," Tom answered. Then he demanded, "Jack, where's Curly?"

Jack looked his boss in the eyes and answered, "I believe he's dead, sir. A steer gored him and his horse when the storm passed overhead. Curly tried to jump away, and me and Ty tried to rope him off, but he went under before we could do much more than that. I'll keep on looking, but if he's gone-my condolences."

Orr's face turned an alarming shade of red and he screamed at his men, "You boys—keep an eye out for Curly Buck. He might be washed up somewhere... hurry!" Facing Jack again he added, "Goddammit! He was right, Jack. He flat knew that this river would be the death of him, but I made him cross anyway."

Ballard shook his head. "No sir. It weren't nothin' you did. It was a freak storm that blew up outta nowhere. I think the stragglers were more blowed-up by the dead girl than the storm. Curly Buck just ran outta luck."

Orr frowned. "Dead girl? What dead girl?"

Jack realized that Orr, of course, had been at least a half mile ahead when Sally Lloyd made her bizarre entrance and Tom would not have known about it until they met up again after the crossing. Explaining, Jack informed his boss about the prostitute's sudden appearance and Orr shook his head in awe.

He said, "You know, right before we left Bandera, Curly and I went to a local hole in the wall for a drink and so he could give his gal a kiss goodbye. Her name's Consuela, or Connie, and she works with a hoo-doo woman called Madame Fortune."

Orr pulled his hat off and wiped at his face. He tried to make it look like he was wiping sweat away, but Jack knew he was wiping tears of sorrow from his eyes. Continuing, Tom said, "Funny thing is, Curly seemed pretty shook up at what that crazy old bat, Madame Fortune, had to say—something about staying away from golden hair and rushing waters…"

His eyes got big. Turning to Jack, Tom asked, "Have you seen that weird necklace Curly was wearing there for a while?"

Jack nodded. "Yup. It's hangin' up by the head of his cot. The boys were giving him so much guff for wearing it, he couldn't stand the embarrassment anymore."

Tom's shoulders slumped. "Dammit—this is going from bad to worse in a hurry." Looking at Jack he said, "The storm has blown over and we need to find our dead, do some burying, and gather up what's left of the herd. You'll help me out, right Jack?"

Ballard nodded and answered, "Of course, sir. I'll set us up a couple of teams to find and bring back our dead… although it looks like it's already being done."

Tom turned around and looked toward the north beach. He saw that Hitch and Mateo had pulled a couple of wagons close, most of the hands were poking around along the shoreline and several dead bodies were lined up, side by side on the sand.

Gazing at Jack, Tom asked, "If worse comes to worst, will you stand in for Curly as my second until we get to Dodge City? I hate to ask it of ya, knowing you don't care for a leadership position, but I'll need help to keep the boys in line…"

He sighed, and continued, "Funny thing about a broken crew—sometimes when a drive goes wrong like mine's done, the cowboys will turn into crooks just to make sure they get paid for their misery. These boys won't know or believe that their fair wages are already waiting for them in Dodge City. Too much toil and trouble and their greed will take over their common sense… seen it happen before"

Jack shifted in his saddle. He really just wanted to get paid for his work and see the back-side of this drive but he knew Tom was right. Nodding, he said, "Yes, sir. I will be your second, at least until we hit Dodge City. But, can I make a suggestion?"

Orr squinted and asked, "What?"

Jack answered, "If I was you, I'd be having me a sit-down with these boys as soon as possible, and as soon as I got their attention, I'd tell 'em that their wages are waiting on your arrival and inform them that your presence is *required* for the funds to be released."

Orr frowned thoughtfully, and then shrugged. "Actually, my wife and one of my trusted farm hands will be waiting on my arrival and have been instructed to pay the cowboys wages whether I'm alive or not. But what those boys don't know won't hurt 'em, neither." He shook his head and snorted. "If this ain't a dog eat dog world…"

Jack Ballard grinned past the pain and swelling that throbbed in his cheeks. "Yessir, it surely is, but every good dog has his day, doesn't he?"

## Chapter Thirty-Five

IT TOOK TWO DAYS TO RECOVER THEIR MISSING MEN AND TO gather as much of the herd together as possible. There were still about 3900 beeves left, which was fortunate, but the victory seemed hollow after losing their comrades.

In all, they'd lost seven men; three dead, like Curly Buck, whom they'd finally found skewered in a tangle of mesquite, Winston Mackey—drowned and Teddy Williams—apparently expired from a terrible blow to the head. Another four men were so badly injured they'd need to be transported in the wagons as quickly as possible to seek medical help. There were plenty of wounded animals, as well, and Latigo and Yellow Bird set to tending them as tenderly as if they were their own kin.

Their gear was scattered all over hell but after two days of back-breaking and mournful labor, they were finally ready to go—destination Doan's Store. There was, apparently, a decent outpost in the middle of nowhere about thirty miles further, and Orr needed to replenish the goods they'd lost like; food, pots, pans, blanket rolls, leather gear, etc. The more urgent need, however, was medical help and Tom had learned there was a doctor living close to the outpost.

It was another two-day drive but finally they pulled into a tiny modicum of society, although many of the hands were disappointed. Doan's "Store" wasn't much more than a couple of shabby adobe huts, built side-by-side with a corral attached to the south-end of the buildings. Still, Jack saw a water-well, which was an immediate necessity.

He, Tom Orr and Hitch had left the Drago brothers in charge of the herd and now rode up to the store with their two wagons after dropping their wounded off with the local saw-bones. They stepped down off the wagons and walked through a burlap flap that covered the front door.

Surprisingly, the hut was larger than expected and the front-half of the building was stuffed to the rafters with all manner of gear—shovels, rakes, bridles, harnesses, ropes of every gauge and length, pots, pans, chain, horseshoes, clothing and foot wear.

On the floor and piled on shelves were buckets and barrels of wheat, lard, pickles, eggs, sugar, coffee, flour and molasses. Behind the counter hung a bloody cattle carcass, a dismembered sheep, two hogs and about a half dozen freshly killed chickens. It was a wonderful bounty and weirdly unlikely—rising up out of the sere Texas desert like a dream.

Immediately, Hitch produced a long list of needed items and Tom, having money in the bank but currently cash poor, got ready to strike a hard bargain. Meanwhile,

Jack wandered toward the back of the building where he could hear the sound of muted voices.

Stepping between two barrels of pickles, he saw several small tables set up close to a long wooden bench behind which a portly man was filling drink orders. "Howdy! What can I getcha?" he said with an almost toothless smile.

Jack smiled back, and said, "I got some work to do out front but maybe me and my friends will step in for a nip before we leave."

The balding man answered, "Whal, I got plenty of whiskey, a little beer and some coffee when you're ready. Plus, give it a coupla hours and the beans will be ready... got lotsa pork-back in it!"

Jack gave a slight wave and when he turned around to help Tom and Hitch with their order, he saw four grim-looking fellows seated around one of the back tables. Three of them were dressed very nicely with white shirts, vests, black pants and neckties. The other man was older and dressed more casually in canvas pants, a striped over-shirt and a flop hat. Two of them were drinking whiskey but two others held steaming cups of coffee in front of their faces.

They were all tough-looking customers and judging by the dim glimmer of metal on one of the men's vest, Jack reckoned he was looking at a well-heeled posse. The man with the star called out, "Hello. What's your business here?"

Jack was suddenly nervous and also offended. Even in Texas, strangers were usually polite, and certainly not snoops. It just made sense not to rile up men you didn't know from Adam. Still, the stout and handsome man carried a self-assured grin and seemed friendly enough.

Jack answered, "Just a cow-hand looking to re-supply our cattle drive—the Triple T out of Bandera—after we were hit by that twister aways back. We're heading up to Dodge City."

The men exchanged glances and one of them, a taller gentleman with dark hair and a luxurious mustache said, "Heard about that storm—you suffer any casualties?"

Jack nodded. "Yessir, three dead and four more wounded. Just dropped them off at the doc's place."

The leader spoke again, "Sorry about the blunt question. My name's Masterson-Sheriff Bat Masterson out of Dodge City. This here is Marshal Virgil Earp and his brother, Wyatt. Turning to his left, he pointed to the other man in their party, "And this is Bill Tilghman… one of our deputies. There is a bad group of horse thieves prowlin' these parts and we're trying to track 'em down."

He took a deep pull off his glass of amber and added, "You men better stay sharp as you head north, right? The boys we're hunting down are killers of men and woman as well as horse thieves. Also, y'all know you're heading into Indian country, right?"

Jack nodded. "Yes sir, the Cheyenne/Arapaho Reservation. We'll be careful, I can promise you that much."

Masterson smiled. "That's good. Last thing I want to do is end this chase by pickin' your bones up for buryin.'"

Jack saluted and stepped back between the two barrels to help load the newly acquired supplies.

## Chapter Thirty-Six

JACK AND HIS COMPANIONS *DID* STEP INTO THE BAR AREA for a nip after loading their supplies but, by then, the posse had moved on. They each took a drink and Tom purchased six bottles of whiskey—most of his stash was gone for having used it to ease his injured cowboy's discomfort. Also, on occasion, he liked to reward his crew with a well-earned toast.

They rode back to the herd, which was situated along a small stream and Jack saw that the camp seemed to be in good working order. He noticed Con and Tyson Drago watching their approach and frowned as Ty spat on the ground in disgust, before mounting his horse and riding off.

Jack shook his head and, not for the first time, wondered if he was going to cross swords, so to speak, with that boy before the drive was finished. Tom had noticed Ty's actions, and murmured, "That's one hombre I won't be sorry to see gone."

As usual, though, Conrad was friendly as he hailed the

two wagons. "Howdy," he called out. "Looks like you got the goods we need... most of the crew would kill for a pot of coffee."

Tom nodded. "Yessir, got coffee, and something else to ease their itch..." He grinned as he pulled a full bottle of hooch from a wooden crate situated between himself and Jack on the bench seat of his wagon.

Con's eyes got big and he replied, "Hoo-wee! That'll sure go down good, fer sure."

Tom said, "Tell the boys to come and help us unpack the supplies, and after they're done, they can each have two pulls off the bottle. I want them—all of us—to get some grub and good rest before we hit the Reservation, which should be tomorrow afternoon."

Con tipped his hat and rode off to gather up what remained of their crew. They had started out with thirty-two hands and were now down to twenty. Not a lot of help, but the herd was diminished as well as the human crew. Tom and Jack had discussed the situation and agreed that they were close enough to Dodge City, they should be able to handle the herd until they hit the stock pens.

*That is, if nothing more goes wrong,* Jack thought with an uneasy grimace. He'd been in on four cattle drives in his life, and he had never seen a drive so bedeviled as this one. Oh, there were usually a number of problems in every long drive, but this one was reaching epic propor-tions, and Jack couldn't wait to get shut of the whole enterprise.

They spent the rest of the evening with full bellies and the warm glow of whiskey to sooth their souls and the next morning, they were raring to hit the trail. The weather was mild and the air crisp and clean, as if the storm had washed summer's residue away to make room for autumn.

They were traveling on a wide swatch of trampled grass and dirt on what was referred to as the "Western Trail." The crew saw numerous cold campfires and even a little rubble left behind from other trail drives and were not surprised when they came upon a large, hand-written sign that stated,

**Beware!**
**You are now entering the**
**Cheyenne~Arapaho Reservation**

Jack, who was now riding with Mateo at the head of the drive, said to Tom Orr, "Well, that's handy to know."

Orr nodded. "Yup. Better call a stop and get these boys geared-up."

Tom, Jack and Mateo managed to bring the drive to a halt and Orr ordered the hands who normally carried guns to load their firearms and told the rest of the cowboys to go to his wagon for additional fire power. Then, he said, "Be ready for anything. It's about a two-day drive across this land, and we should be all right, but we also heard that Sheridan's Army is battling the Kiowa, Southern Cheyenne and Comanche which means that the Indians around here are all riled up and ready to make war on any comers. So, stay sharp!"

They rolled on, knowing there were likely hostiles all around them and a fair stretch between here and Dodge City. Orr was feeling positive—he figured there was just no way anything more could happen—to his mind, more misfortune was simply against all odds.

Jack, however, being of gloomier disposition and more prone to worry, found himself holding his breath against the next unfortunate incident. He was figuring out the trail going north and mentally ticking off the next few stops they'd likely hit before crossing the Arkansas River into Dodge City when he heard a distant shout of alarm.

Looking to his right, he saw five men trotting briskly their way. They were obviously Mexicans—their way of sitting a horse, their concho-laden saddles and bridles—their low-crowned hats announced their identity as clearly as an engraved calling card.

Trotting up to Tom, he could hear his boss swearing in frustration. "Damn it, Jack. We're so far north by now, I thought we'd shaken off any interference from the Mexican federales, but they must really have a bee in their bonnet about old Mateo..." Raising his voice. He called out, "Mateo, come here, quick!"

They both saw Mateo spur his horse their way and Tom added, "I *did* have enough money to buy them off, but I thought we'd left them in our dust and spent all I had—pretty much—at Doan's store. Now, I'm broke, and those guys are gonna demand something to let Mateo go free."

Jack shrugged, although in truth it stung. "Boss, I got almost fifty bucks in my boot—will that help?"

Tom Orr stared at Jack with gratitude in his eyes. "Sure would, Jack. That might just do the trick. I would pay ya back just as soon as we hit Dodge City..."

Jack nodded. "Done, then."

Mateo trotted up to them and Orr said, "Looks like

your old friends have arrived to collect their due. I got a plan, but just in case, I want you to go hide in Hitch's wagon."

Mateo sighed, and said, "I'm sorry, senor Tom. I did not mean to bring trouble on this drive."

Orr shook his head, and said, "No trouble, Mateo. Just make yourself scarce while Jack and I try to sort this out. Go!"

Mateo galloped away to hide in the cook wagon as Tom and Jack turned their horses to face their incoming guests.

## Chapter Thirty-Seven

CON AND TY DRAGO WATCHED WITH INTEREST AND SOME anxiety. They knew about Mateo and his trouble with the Federales, and normally wouldn't give a fig whether the man was killed outright or dragged away to face a lifetime in a Mexican prison.

But they, themselves, had keen interest in this particular undertaking and if Tom Orr paid the Mexicans off with part of his herd, that would cut into *their* bottom-line. *That will not do*, Con thought with an aggravated frown.

He turned toward his brother and said, "If it looks like things are going south for Orr, I want you to take as many of those beaners out as possible. I'll do the same—working left to right."

Ty nodded. "Yeah, cain't have those hombres cutting into our profit margin, cuz as soon as we hit Dodge City our chance to make any more money on this enterprise dries up—right?"

"That's right, Ty. Now's the time to make hay. Also, if it goes thataway, we'll just look like heros trying to save the herd, instead of profiteers. Just wait and see, though. Maybe Orr has something up his sleeve we don't know about. Hate to jump the gun if this can be settled peaceably."

Ty nodded and followed his older brother as Con made his way closer to the confrontation. The five Mexies had come to a stop in front of Orr and the traitor, Jack Ballard. They heard a smattering of English mixed in with a lot of Spanish as the lead Federale quizzed Orr.

The man spoke English reasonably well. "We are looking for a Mexican man named Mateo Gonzales. We have reason to believe he murdered a group of bounty hunters, and we have come to arrest him. Is he with your herd?"

Orr studied the man, whippet-thin with great, drooping mustaches, who was staring past his shoulders at the armed cowboys facing him. Weighing the options in his mind, Tom knew that the numbers were on his side. He figured that the lead Federale could count as well as he did and probably doubted that a shooting match would fall in his favor.

Nodding politely, Orr tested his theory. "My name is Tom Orr, and this is my second, Jack Ballard." He turned around in his saddle, slightly, and then faced the Federale again. "Yup," he said. "Mateo's riding with us. He's been working for me about a year and a half now and I can assure you he has not been on a killing spree… he's been too busy helping me wrestle this herd north from Bandera.

The lead Federale, whose name was Juan Esposito,

introduced himself and then frowned thoughtfully. "But senor, we found those bounty hunters—Mexican citizens —dead along the trail your herd took to get here. How do you explain that?"

Orr shrugged. "There are many hazards along the way, right? Indians, storms... why do you assume our Mateo played a part in their deaths?"

Esposito raised an eyebrow. "Perhaps you think we are estupido, si? That we can't tell that those men died from multiple gunshot wounds fired from American pistols? Please..."

Knowing the game was up, Orr shrugged. "Okay, it's true that I can't keep an eye on every single man in an outfit this size. Maybe there *was* gunplay and Mateo took part in the fracas. But I know the young man in question. I also know that the charges brought against him were unfair. If you and your men have any honor at all, you know that what he did was done in defense of his poor mamma and was only right and just."

There was a flurry of discussion amongst Esposito's fellow lawmen at Orr's words. Tom couldn't really understand what the men were whispering but Jack heard quite plainly; "That's not the point!" one man said, and another said, "I've been saying the same thing all along! Young Mateo did the only honorable thing—the same thing anyone of us would do if we were in his place!"

Juan held up a hand and his companions fell silent. "Por favor," he sighed. "whether Mateo is guilty, or not, we must have recompense. I have my own bosses to contend with, and if there is no compensation for our long ride into Texas, it will be my head on a stake, si?"

Orr had been waiting for this. Staring Esposito in the eye, he asked, "May I reach into my shirt pocket?"

The Mexican leader frowned and put his hand close to his pistol and his comrades followed suit. Both Orr and Ballard wondered if their discussion had suddenly come to a violent end, but Esposito said, "Yes—very slowly and carefully."

Tom nodded and pulled a wad of cash out of his shirt pocket. "This is all we have—and that's the truth. A big storm moved in about sixty miles back and we suffered great losses, including most of our supplies. I had to spend almost all my cash paying doctors and re-supplying. But here's one hundred and twenty dollars... will that help make up for your time and efforts?"

Esposito stared at the proffered cash and was relieved. He too, felt sympathy for Mateo Gonzales, and knew how a bad Patron could ruin a person's life. It had happened to his own Papa and Mamma, and almost to him before he found his way into the Mexican police force. Still, he had to justify his actions and this cash would appease his bosses back home.

He smiled, and answered, "Si, that will help. Gracias." He took the notes from Orr's hand and stuffed them into his coat pocket. Looking around at his men, Esposito made a slight hand movement, and the men turned their horses around to face back the way they came.

The Federale spoke, "We will go home now, senor. But know this—there *will* be other posses looking to profit from Mateo's death. My men and me... we think the way you do, but many others will not care—if his capture lines their pockets. Truly, in the long run, the best thing for him would be to come home, find a good lawyer and plead his case."

Esposito looked past Tom's shoulder as though he wished he could speak directly to the man in question. "There are many, I know, who would stand as witness to his innocence, including me and my compatriots. Until then, however, the hunt for his body and soul will continue."

With those words, Esposito tipped his flat-brimmed hat and the Mexican federales rode away south.

———

CONRAD DRAGO SIGHED IN RELIEF. He and his brother had managed to squirrel away about $5000 on the illicit sale of Orr's beeves but he wanted more before the game was up in Dodge City.

He knew that his bosses had profited from the theft of Orr's cattle, but Con had managed to swing other—more private—sales, and that was going to come to an end soon. As soon as they reached Dodge City, he and his brother had been ordered to leave—immediately.

He itched to be a part of Jack Ballard's final moments, but he knew that his bosses were correct. If worse came to worst, and the Blue Sash members were arrested for Ballard's murder, the society wanted no one around who could, conveniently, shift the blame.

*Still,* Con thought resentfully, *me and Ty was the ones who had to do all the dirty work while my bosses get to revel in the glory of revenge!*

Seeing the cowboys moving out and hearing the cattle moan their disapproval, Con wondered how he might arrange for a terrible accident to befall his enemy. Something that could never be traced back to him or his brother. Something horrible, painful, shameful.

Con smiled slightly, kicked his horse's flanks and went to do his part in moving the herd northeast into Kansas. Anyone watching would have wondered at the evil gleam in Drago's eyes.

## Chapter Thirty-Eight

THE DRIVE MOVED SLOWLY UP THE WESTERNMOST TRAIL that skirted the Cheyenne~Arapaho Reservation. Once in a while Jack, Mateo and Tom Orr saw the silent silhouette of a mounted figure on a distant ridgeline or the upper crags of some stony outcropping.

"Indians, checking us out," Jack murmured.

"Si," Mateo agreed.

Orr, who could practically feel the hatred steaming off those silent sentinels like smoke, muttered, "What do you think, Jack? Are they gonna attack?"

Jack shook his head. "Doubt it. They wouldn't challenge us alone like that. Still, if we see more than one or two riding together, we'd best get ready for a fight."

Orr frowned. He hated to be at the mercy of others, and this silent test of nerves was wearing him down. Twice more he and his men caught a glimpse of their watchers and finally Tom pulled his reins back, stopping his horse. "This cat and mouse game is driving me crazy," he said. "What do you two think we should do... just brazen it out?"

Jack shook his head. "Nah, I think they're planning an attack. Maybe on us or just the herd, but either way they're dogging us too much just to satisfy their curiosity."

Tom grimaced. "That's what I was thinkin', too. Here's what I want to do—how 'bout I ride back to the herd and send a couple of men with rifles back to you for a scouting mission? I can only spare a couple of bodies because I need the rest of my men to guard our flanks. If those injuns are planning to heist my beeves, I'll be losing money on this drive-so much money, I'll lose my shirt and maybe my hands' shirts, too."

Jack studied the terrain and figured the odds. Nodding, he said, "Sounds good, boss. Why don't you send Con and Ty on ahead? They're both keen shots and we may be in for a tussle."

Tom looked worried. "Am I doing the right thing? I don't want to lose you men, but I'm equally worried over the stock—God help me."

Both Jack and Mateo objected. "No, Senor Tom, you are doing the only thing. I, too, believe those natives are going to attack and this way, Jack and me and..." he grimaced with distaste, "those other men can fight off an attack with our guns!"

Jack had been about to say the same thing but subsided with a small smile. Mateo had just answered for him. Tom studied both their faces and then sighed. "Okay then, you two wait and I'll send the Drago boys up here to help you out."

He turned his horse around and took off at a sharp trot. Jack and Mateo stepped off their horses and took the opportunity to water themselves first and then fill their hats with water for their mounts. Then, they walked their horses to a rocky cliff-face and sat down in the shade to wait.

About a half an hour later, they heard the sound of hoofbeats and displaced rocks and gravel as the Drago brothers rode up the trail. "Howdy!" Con drawled with a grin. "Heard we're gonna roust us a few red injuns."

Jack stood up and said, "Well, hopefully not. But the signs aren't good. Looks like they want to pick a fight and we're going to try and stop that from happening."

Con looked down and snarled, "Ain't nobody gonna come between me and my bottom-line, Jack. If those savages want these beeves, they'll have to go through me and my brother to get 'em!"

Jack felt another thrill of uncertainty regarding the Drago boys and their motives. Usually, he felt at ease around Con, at least, but the way he'd just spoken made Ballard feel as if Con and Ty considered Tom Orr's herd their own, making him wonder, yet again, if they'd had something to do with the drive's earlier losses.

Still, he was in charge of this maneuver and he said, "Okay, I want us to split up as soon as we leave this crag and make our way down into the valley on the other side of this cliff. Con, you and Ty move to the left and Mateo and I will go to the right. Mainly, this is a scouting mission so don't make a fuss until we get the lay of the land, okay?"

Ty opened his mouth as if to argue but Con interrupted, "Sure thing, Jack. Are you riding in or walking your horse?"

Jack replied, "I'm walking in. We don't know anything

yet, ya know. There could be an army of them, for all we know."

Con grinned. "Ty and me—we'll follow your lead. I'd hate to be pin cuchioned by a host of Cheyenne or Arapaho before we even got a chance to fight."

Leaving their horses tied-up, Jack and Mateo moved ahead to a cut in the rock wall and peered down at the valley below. Jack could hear the Drago boys coming up behind them and moving to the left. Moving slowly, Jack pulled his hat low over his brow and crouched down, feeling rather than seeing Mateo do the same thing.

Sure enough, Jack saw at least fifty or sixty braves gathered together in a confabulation, just four or five hundred yards below them. Hardly daring to breathe, Jack silently motioned for Mateo to back away and he tried to catch the Drago's attention as well, but they were gazing at the Indians with dark fury.

He backed slowly away thinking that he and his crew needed to ride back to the herd-pronto—and convince Tom to back off and contemplate their options against this apparent war-party He was also hoping they'd have a chance to reconsider their current route before the Indians spotted them, stuck as they were on the side of this hill.

Jack made his way to the cut, Mateo close behind him, and was thinking that they were all so dirty and dust-covered, perhaps they were blending into the landscape when he heard a hoarse shout. Peering through two large boulders, he saw a number of braves shouting and pointing at Tyson Drago who, for some reason, had stood up and was now displaying himself to the natives with brazen disregard to his own health.

Brandishing his rifle, Ty hollered, "Come and get me, you red skunks! Come on and taste a bellyful of lead!'

Jack winced even as Mateo gasped. "Mio Dios, what is he doing?"

Jack saw Con try to drag his brother to cover, but the kid had lost his composure entirely and now started to shoot at the Indians, who seemed to side-step his shots with almost supernatural ease.

Jack dragged himself through the cut and jumped to the side so Mateo could join him in relative safety. Then, he turned around again and looked for Ty and Con. Con was still trying to calm his brother down, but Ty was having none of it.

Then, just as Jack was about to give it up and mount his horse, he saw an arrow plow its way, from front to back, through Ty's neck. His shouts were instantly cut-off, and Con's anguished cry rose into the air.

Knowing no one could survive such a killing blow, he shouted, "Con, let's go! I know you're sad, but I don't want you to die up here! Now, come on!"

## Chapter Thirty-Nine

CON HELD HIS DYING BROTHER IN HIS ARMS AND SAW TYSON choke and gasp through the blood filling his mouth. He was sucking air like a fish of out water, while his limbs trembled, and his heels beat a tattoo on the hard-packed earth. His eyes were wide and scared, and he tried to say something but then his gaze became fixed, and his jaw fell slack.

Con cried out in pain, but he heard Jack hollering, "Con, Let's go!"

He stared one last time at his beloved baby brother and then jumped to his feet as arrows pocked the rocks and scree around him. He looked over his shoulder and saw that a number of braves were scaling the hillside and getting closer every second.

He threw caution to the wind then, opting for haste rather than stealth as, obviously, he'd been spotted. Standing up straight, Con ran all-out for the cut on the hillside. He saw both Jack and Mateo waiting for him, urging him on, when he was punched from behind with a sickening thud.

Knowing he'd caught an arrow, Con staggered through the rocks and fell at the hooves of Jack's horse. His whole body felt numb, but for the nausea crawling up his throat. Groaning, he reached a hand up and felt it grasped. Then, as stars filled his eyes and a high ringing filled his ears he was on his own horse and galloping down the other side of the hill toward the herd.

He passed out then and wasn't aware when his horse was pulled to a stop, and he was tied onto his saddle. He slept off and on as the trio rushed to safety and he dreamed of his brother's face.

———

JACK, Mateo and Con's hunched-over body approached at a dead gallop and Tom knew the herd was in big trouble. *Also, where the hell is Ty?* he wondered uneasily, fearing the worst.

Jack and Rebel skidded to a stop, and Ballard shouted, "Tom! Circle the herd and tell the boys to get ready. We're in for a fight… also, get Hitch and Levi up here. Con's got an arrow in his right shoulder."

Tom immediately ordered the cowhands to work and turned back to Ballard. "Where's Ty?"

"We lost him, Jack. Those Indians are camped out just behind that butte, yonder." He pointed to the east and Tom's eyes got big at how close the hostiles were to him and his herd.

Jack continued, "I have no idea what got into that boy, boss, but we were at the top of the hill, surveilling and pretty well-hidden, when he stood up and started screaming and shooting at them." Jack shook his head so as to not disremember the event. "Tom, it was like he just went loco of a sudden. It surely was a suicide—for all of us. It's a miracle we got away at all, but now we've tipped our hand, and they're coming to make war."

Tom groaned. "How many! Do we got a chance, at all?"

Jack's eyes were bleak as he answered, "There's always a chance, boss, but it's gonna be tough. There are, at least, fifty of them—maybe more."

Tom sighed. "I declare—I've been cursed, and so have my men." He stared at the ground for a moment, then looked up. "Still, we gotta try, right?"

Jack nodded. "Yessir, we do."

Just then, Hitch and young Levi, who had shown a solid talent in the healing arts showed up with the wagon. Con had already been lowered to the ground and they could all see that the arrow protruding from the back of Con's shoulder had sunk deep but was still lodged firmly in his body.

Jack grimaced, knowing it was going to be a tough surgery. It would have been better if the arrow had gone clean through, but now they would need to pull the dart out, and who knew what vital human equipment might come out with it?

Con was a big man and it took all four of them to lift him into the back of the wagon and place him on his belly. Jack stood for a moment and watched as Hitch and Levi cut Con's shirt off and poured whiskey over the wound. Then, after administering the blessed, newly purchased laudanum, they set-to, and Jack climbed on Rebel and went in search of Tom, who was yelling at his men to move the herd as close to Hitch's wagon as possible.

Jack joined in and soon most of the herd, including the remuda was in a tight circle milling about the wagons which were situated in the middle. Jack studied the group he rode with and felt proud. A cowboy was posted every fifty-yards or so, and each of them were armed to the teeth. The cook was holding his shotgun, Latigo held his rifle, and even the Oriental laundresses were armed and ready to fight. Yellow Bird stood by a skittish young colt, whispering in its ear, and out of the whole group, he, alone, remained unarmed.

*These men and women are not warriors,* he thought, *but they are game roosters, for sure,* and he vowed to protect them, even if he lost his life in the process.

———

CON WAS LOST *in a dream of blood and fire. He was chasing Ty through some strange, unearthly field, and calling out, "Ty! Tyson, wait up!" but the boy just kept running, turning around occasionally to laugh at him and gesture a "hurry-up!"*

*That boy had always been about half-crazy... too many twigs and branches mingling together from the same family tree, Con reckoned, but this was ridiculous! If he couldn't catch up to Ty, the boy would be lost forever on that far-distant horizon.*

*"No!" Con hollered. "I can't see you... wait!" But Ty had vanished into a wall of smoke, and then Jack Ballard was standing over him with a wicked grin. He held a flaming-hot poker in his hand and he snarled, "Hold on, Con, this is gonna hurt." And then he howled in laughter as Con screamed.*

*Jack plunged the poker into his shoulder and the pain was so excruciating, so over-whelming, Con thought the flames of hell were licking at him with greedy, demon tongues. He groaned with fear and fury as the poker was pulled out, and vowed revenge against the man who was torturing him and had gotten his little brother killed.*

Con had no idea that he was also afflicted with the seeds of madness that had been passed down in his family from generation to generation. Ty had been ill-equipped to hide his psychosis', but Con had managed to maintain a calmer disposition, thus hiding the deeply-rooted insanity shared with his grandfather, father and uncles.

Passed out now, Con looked for but failed to catch a glimpse of his little brother. He did decide, however, deep in his subconscious mind, that Jack Ballard—the betrayer, the traitor had somehow arranged Ty's demise with cold and calloused efficiency, and he vowed the darkest revenge.

———

AFTER PULLING the heavy war arrow out of Con's shoulder, and watching him fall deeply asleep, Hitch and Levi looked at each other and hoped for the best. There was really no way of knowing whether they'd helped the man or made things worse by removing the arrow. Still, they'd managed to stem the bleeding and had cleaned the wound up as best they could.

The rest, Hitch knew, was up to God. "Okay, kid." he sighed. "Better grab that rifle. I think we got company coming, and soon."

## Chapter Forty

AN HOUR PASSED—AND THEN TWO AS THE TRIPLE T BOYS waited for the Indians to attack. The heat rose up off the ground in waves and to make matters worse, the flies chose that moment to descend from the heavens above.

There were your common variety flies buzzing, hissing, hovering, and then landing on every exposed inch of the cowhand's sweaty flesh—a maddening nuisance, but not dangerous. However, things got more hazardous as horseflies and bees with bared teeth and stingers joined the flies to make life almost unbearable.

In addition, the smell of the herd animals bunched up together as they circled the wagons made breathing an exercise in futility. Cow hair, horse sweat, and dust filled the human's nostrils and one of the laundresses trapped inside the herd gasped and fainted. As the minutes ticked by, and Jack swatted at yet another stinging insect, he studied the distant hillside with stoic resentment.

This slow stand-off was, no doubt, by design on the Indians' part. A sort of psychological warfare was being waged he knew and, so far, the natives were winning the battle. Frustrated, Jack wished they would stop playing around and attack—just to get shut of this waiting game.

Finally, whooping and hollering, two fighting braves came from behind them. They approached, brandishing their spears but two rifle blasts shattered the air and one of the braves toppled from his horse—dead. The other Indian threw his spear but turned his pony around and fled back from whence he came.

Within seconds, a group of four fighters came from the east. These men carried spears as well, but two of them held bows and arrows. The riders in front brandished their spears but split away as the two behind them stopped their horses, took aim and shot two cowboys stationed by that section of the rear guard.

Jack frowned, gritting his teeth as the two cowhands fell to the ground, screaming in mortal agony. Meanwhile, although the arrow-wielding braves wheeled their horses to flee, Hitch and Orr took aim and fired their rifles. One of the braves howled in pain, but both rode away, disappearing from sight.

Then, there was a break in the action which allowed the men to run and fetch their wounded friends. There was little comfort in it, though, as both of the young men had died from the heavy war-arrows.

Each of Orr's men checked their weapons and ammunition as Jack and Rebel paced back and forth in front of the herd. He didn't think this would be a battle of attrition... most Indians didn't conduct guerilla warfare. Rather, they used superior numbers to over-whelm their prey.

Honestly, he thought, he and the crew might survive

this slow pot-shot affair, but he doubted they could over-come the Indians numbers. He sensed this was just a warm-up, however, and the natives would soon attack in full-force.

Another forty-five minutes passed and suddenly they all heard a distant war-whoop from the east. Then they saw a great cloud of dust rising on the horizon. Tom Orr, sensing the fearful tension in his cowhand's breasts, turned his horse around and said, "Hold steady, boys. Remember, we have two crack shots on our side—Jack and Mateo. I'm not a bad hand with a rifle either, nor will Hitch fail to drop his fair share of savages."

He lifted a shaking hand, removed his hat and wiped sweat from his forehead. "Just keep shootin' and whatever you do, don't turn tail and run away from cover! They'll pick you off like ducks in a barrel."

Turning to the front again, he muttered, "Well, Jack, here goes nuthin.'"

Jack nodded slightly and watched as the distant hazy shape of Indian's and their horses emerged from the cloud of dust. Heart sinking, he knew that the next few minutes would probably be his last on earth. He understood that his previous estimate of the Indian's numbers was grossly inadequate. There were now, at least, a hundred-probably closer to two hundred—fighting braves cresting the horizon and heading their way at a full gallop.

Jack's chest grew heavy with unexpected-and unwanted—regret. He hadn't been aware until now that he was missing human companionship—and all it entailed—in his life-long quest to right the wrongs visited upon him and his during the war.

He hadn't realized that he secretly desired a woman

and children of his own. He didn't know how much he longed for a family and friends and deep-rooted ties to his community... and how he wished to cleave to love before he died.

And now all those secret desires, hidden from him until this very minute, cried out in anguish as death bore down on him on with unshod hooves. He blinked back the tears that threatened his courage and lifted his rifle in defiance. Then he heard Mateo say, "Senor Jack, look!"

He'd been sighting down the barrel of his rifle, but he followed Mateo's pointing finger, and saw Yellow Bird walking slowly toward the encroaching army. He walked hunched over and shuffling like a sand crab, but his bearing was proud as he held up his hand in the universal greeting of the Plains Indians.

"My God, what's he doin?" Tom whispered.

"Don't know, boss, but see? They are slowing down to palaver," Jack answered.

And, sure enough, the Indians had stopped and were now addressing the oldster with dignified courtesy. Jack and his companions watched open-mouthed as many of the braves stepped down off their hoses and went to grasp Yellow Bird's hand and hug his frail shoulders.

The meeting went on for a few more minutes and then the old chief stepped away from the group and headed back in their direction. Yellow Bird walked slowly, and Jack could see the enigmatic smile on his friend's face.

Yellow Bird walked up to where Jack sat his horse and said, "I have made a trade."

Tom opened his mouth to speak, worried perhaps that this "trade" involved his cattle, but Jack put a hand out and Orr shut his mouth.

Staring back and forth between Jack and Orr, Yellow Bird continued. "I have traded myself—along with fifty steers. This will appease the war party, and you will be allowed to pass through reservation land unmolested."

Orr looked confused. "Well, what's the rub?"

It was the chief's turn to looked confused. "Rub? I do not know, but they will make war if you do not release me-your prisoner." He grinned and winked.

"Prisoner!" Tom blurted, indignant. "Why, I've been paying you fair and squ…"

Again, Jack interrupted as respectfully as he knew how. "Tom, he don't mean no disrespect; he's lying… playing a trick, but doing us a big favor. Trading himself back to his own people will be of great benefit to him, see. They think he's one of the 'big chiefs', which in a way, he is. This way, he retains his honor and can be with his own people while we can make off with our scalps, and most of your herd intact."

Yellow Bird was following their discussion and he grinned as Tom's eyes grew wide with understanding. Sensing Tom's change of heart, Mateo said, "Senor Yellow Bird, I'll will go and fetch your things, si?"

Yellow Bird nodded and stared over at where Latigo watched the proceedings. Then, he lifted a hand in farewell as the big Negro man returned his gesture and walked over to meet Mateo.

It didn't take long to gather the old man's belongings, but when Mateo returned, he was leading the sorrel colt Yellow Bird had gentled by a good harness. Latigo, hollered, "Mr Orr! You can take that hoss outta my share, okay? Yellow Bird's the only one can ride him, anyway."

Orr sighed and nodded even as fifty cattle were cut

from the herd and started trotting east toward the Indian army. He reached in his pocket and tried to give Yellow Bird the rest of his wages, but the old man shook his head, and said, "This horse is a fine gift and the only payment I desire. I might even trade him for a beautiful young wife!"

Tom grinned and nodded. He knew that he and his outfit had gotten off easy and, but for the grace of God and one wiley, old one-eyed Injun, the day would have been lost. Sighing in relief, he waved goodbye and rode back to the cook wagons.

Yellow Bird mounted his horse as nimbly as any youngster and rode up close to Jack. "Go easy, my young friend. Lay down the ghosts of your past and live as your forefathers intended. Find yourself a good woman and let her warm your bed. Have many children and rejoice in this life, or the gods will grow impatient with you."

He put a gnarled hand on Ballard's shoulder, adding, "Once again, I want to thank you helping me bury my granddaughter so many years ago. We are now even, eh?"

Jack nodded, "Yes, grandfather, we are. Go and be at peace."

Then, with a fond smile, Yellow Bird tapped the young horse's flanks, and Jack watched as the wizened old Indian joined his tribe and they galloped away, out of sight.

## Chapter Forty-One

TOM ORR DECIDED TO MOVE OUT AS QUICKLY AS POSSIBLE although it was now late afternoon. He and his hands were still rattled by their close call with the Cherokee nation and they hoped to reach the Arkansas border by nightfall, which was still hours away.

As soon as the cattle started marching west, the flies all but disappeared. A cool breeze had blown-up out of nowhere and the sky was painted in God's pastel pallet.

Jack was moseying along, thinking about the dreadful feelings of regret that had haunted him before the Indians attacked and wondering how he might go about stopping his travels long enough to find a gal and maybe making a family before he got too dang old. He had just figured out that the whole idea was loco when Tom and Mateo rode up.

Orr said, "Just wanted to go over the map a little, okay?"

Jack nodded. "Sure—good to know where we're at."

Tom pulled a well-used map from his vest pocket and

laid it over his saddle horn as Jack and Mateo leaned in to see for themselves. "Okay, we're here abouts," he said, pointing at the western-most border between Texas and Arkansas. "We should be hitting the Camp Supply Spur sometime tomorrow morning. From there we'll head northeast to avoid the Gypsum Hills and then cross over the Canadian into Kansas."

"We stopping for supplies along the way?" Jack asked.

Orr shook his head. "Nah, no need, but I did think we may stop at Deep Hole Crossing. There's a couple of decent saloons and restaurants there plus, several good bath-houses. I'll be seeing my wife in Dodge City the following day and would prefer to hug her as a clean man rather than a rank, old bum."

Jack and Mateo grinned in amusement. They were all filthy, and Jack was sure their collective odor could be smelled from miles away.

Tom continued, "We'll ride until dusk, okay? No hurry, I guess, but now that we're leaving the 'Nation', I'm thinking that rustlers might be a concern. I hope not, by God, but this drive seems to be trouble on the hoof."

Jack nodded, and Mateo tipped his hat and rode off to do a little nighthawking. Jack had just settled in to his thoughts when young Levi rode up with a clatter. Jack was surprised as Hitch rarely let the youngster out of the cook wagon. Still, here he was, looking both scared and determined. "Howdy, sir," the kid said.

Jack smiled and said, "Howdy your own self, Levi. What can I do for ya?"

Levi's freckled face and bright brown eyes stared up at him with concern. He pulled his canteen to his lips, took a draught and answered, "Whal, Hitch and I thought you should know about what Con Drago was saying in his fever dreams. It was purty bad, sir, and mainly all about you being a traitor and all..."

Jack's eyebrows lowered. Being a war veteran, and an officer of good repute, Jack knew that being branded a 'traitor' was one of the worst insults a man could bear. But that war was so long ago by now, he couldn't imagine what kind of sticks and stones could be hurled his way. He stared at Levi and said, "Tell me what Con was sayin', please."

Levi shrugged. "Ya know, of course, that the man has been pretty sick... still is, really. But just after the surgery, when the injuns were headin' in, he started shouting and thrashing around." Levi paused, adding, "Hitch says that's normal, right? But the things he was saying weren't normal, not by a long shot.'

Growing impatient, Jack snapped, "Spit it out, son!"

Levi gulped and said, "Well, sir, he was saying that him and his, um... Blue Sash boy's was gunnin' for ya, and that you was a traitor to the Rebel cause. He was shouting, also, about how him and his brother had led you straight into the arms of justice and how you was gonna be shot down once you reached Dodge City."

Jack's heart stopped for a second and then started thudding heavy in his chest. It had been so many years since he'd fled Lawrence, Kansas after Quantrill's Raiders fired the town and his girlfriend's family farm, he'd almost forgotten his worry and anxiety about putting distance between himself and the Rebel guerillas who'd attacked the town.

Indeed, he'd thought he was entirely forgotten by Quantrill's Raiders in the days that followed their actions in Lawrence and the outlying area. To hear that, somehow, he'd been missed and then labeled a "traitor" was a shock. *Still*, he glared in anger, *I never turned those boys in, or tattled. Why, I never caused them a lick of trouble!*

That was little comfort, though. He had seen many cases of mistaken identity, and charges filed against innocent men and women that were upheld, despite their cries of slander.

Turning to the kid, who looked worried as heck, as if Mr. Jack might blow up in his face, he asked, "Anything else catch your attention, Levi?"

Levi grinned. "Well, this next part concerns Mr. Orr—all of us, I guess—at least Hitch says it do…"

"Well?" Jack urged.

Levi screwed his memory into place and replied, "Old Con started talking about all the money he'd been making from the sale of Mr. Tom's beeves. Says him and Ty have netted over $5000 cutting the herd all the way here from Bandera!"

Jack sat up straight and glanced at Tom who was riding the east side of the herd. "Has Hitch talked to Mr. Orr about this?"

Levi shook his head. "Nah, not yet. I think he's hoping you'll be by his side when he tells the boss. Will you, sir?"

Jack nodded. "I sure will, and you can tell him so. Listen, how is Con doing now, health-wise, I mean?"

Levi looked forlorn. "Oh, he's alive still, but I don't like his color, sir. He looks a little green to me, and the rot is setting in. We have given him everything we have to fight the infection, but I don't think it's doin' much. Now, all he does is lay in back of the wagon, drink whiskey and ask for more 'laudy'.

Jack thought about all the trouble and anxiety the Drago brothers had instigated and how Tom Orr, who had staked everything his family owned on this drive, had been robbed by the Rebel assassins. $5000? *Holy cow*, he thought. *That much money could turn this drive from a loss into a profitable venture!*

"Okay, Levi, thanks for the news. I appreciate it. Ride on back and tell Hitch I'll be there just as soon as I talk with Mr. Orr."

Levi, proud of himself for talking coherently to this intimidating man, tipped his hat and rode back to spell his new foster-father, Hitch Potter, as Jack rode to speak with Tom Orr—and maybe just make his day.

―――――

WHEN JACK and Hitch told Tom about what Con had been saying, his face turned red as a beet. "Why, I shoulda known. Actually, I think I *did* know but old Con is slick as a snake in the grass."

Jack sighed. "He can talk the birds outta the trees, for sure, boss. He had me fooled." He scratched his whiskers, adding, "My question is, where's the cash? Did he stash it along the way, or do you think he has it hidden away in his saddlebags or in the wagon, somewhere?"

Tom's eyes grew big, and without further delay, he and Jack spurred their horses toward the nighthawker's wagon. Jack searched the inside of the wagon but came up empty. Tom, however, shouted out in glee. Sticking his head out the back-flap, Jack asked, "Find something, Tom?"

Orr did a little dance over Con's saddle and saddle

bags which were on the floor boards by the front driver's bench. "Looky here, Jack!" he laughed as Jack stepped up to see for himself.

Tom had pulled two oil-skin sacks out of Con's saddlebags. Bending down to peer inside, Jack saw five or six large rolls of bills, and a wealth of gold and silver coins. Reaching in, both he and Tom counted the money and came up with over thirty-six hundred dollars.

Then, digging around in the undercarriage of the wagon, Jack pulled Ty's saddle bags out and found another two-thousand in coins and draft notes hidden inside. Handing the money to Tom, Jack said, "Your drive is, at least, a financial success, despite all the obstacles in our way, and the lives we lost getting here."

Tom's happy smile faded. He said, "Way I see it, a lot of those losses were caused, in one way or the other, by the Drago brothers!"

He held up a hand, adding, "Oh, I know they had nuthin' to do with the storm, or the Indian attack, but how 'bout that stampede? I know one of them skunks was behind it. Also, there was something hinky about what happened to Mateo and those Mexican bounty hunters. I felt as if Con knew about it but didn't say nuthin' or do anything to help Mateo out."

Jack agreed, and said, "I figured that, too, boss. What do you want to do now... should we hang him as a cattle rustler? We're well within our rights to do so."

Orr looked tempted, but he asked, "How's he doing, physically?"

Jack shrugged. "Not so good, Tom. Hitch thinks he's on his way out, even as we speak."

Tom thought about it for a moment and said, "Well, I

don't hanker after hangin' a man on my own say-so. Let's see what God says about all this, alright? If he's still alive once we reach Dodge City, we'll report what he and his brother done to Sheriff Masterson or Virgil Earp. I heard they don't got no compunctions about hanging cattle rustlers.

## Chapter Forty-Two

THE HERD MOVED SLOWLY-VERY SLOWLY-THROUGH THE prairie dog town just outside of Camp Supply Spur. The tiny beasts were amusing to be sure—sticking their heads up out of their holes to chatter and screech disapproval of the herd's passage like gossips at a church social.

The animal's holes, however, were a hazard to beasts and men alike. One misstep and a cow's leg could break, or a horse might need to be put-down, not to mention human injury or a busted wagon axle.

Finally, they passed by the spur and headed northwest toward Beaver Creek, a tributary of the Canadian River. By mid-afternoon they had crossed the shallow water and could see a small town in the near distance. Deep Hole Crossing—home to saloons, brothels, restaurants and many bath-houses.

Tom, taking pity on the cowhands who'd not been allowed any town visits since starting the drive, sent seventeen men into town first, with strict orders to behave themselves and be back by six o' clock. He, Jack, and Mateo stayed behind to watch the herd.

At a little after six that evening, the hands rode back into camp. Most of them had, obviously, availed themselves of soap and water, and all wore secret smiles of satisfaction. Probably, Jack thought, they'd also helped themselves to the local sporting gals, and eaten a good cafe-bought meal.

Tom thanked the men for their prompt return and asked, "Any trouble?"

Hitch shook his head. "Nah, not for us. But there may be some before the night is through."

Tom frowned. "How so?"

Hitch grinned. "The Longhorn Round-Up Saloon, which is where most of us wet our whistles, is host to none other than Doc Holiday tonight. And, he's fleecing everybody within elbow distance of all their ready cash."

Most of the men on the trail drive had heard of the former dentist and his antics. Many of them thought Holiday was a scamp in the first degree, but some of them, like Jack, who'd met Holiday and exchanged pleasantries more than once, thought the man's illness played a big part in his behavior. It was a way of riding off into death's sunset, not with a whimper, but with a good goddamn.

Hitch removed his hat and stroked his cheeks which were now as smooth as a baby's bottom. He'd apparently hired a barber to rid himself of his chin whiskers. "I'm thinking that there might be some gunplay, except for the fact that that younger of the Earp brother—Wyatt—is sitting shotgun in back of the saloon."

Tom rolled his eyes. "Maybe Jack, Mateo and I will visit the other bar... what's it called?"

"The Deadfall Saloon, sir." This from Levi who had been forced to sit outside on a bench and wait while Hitch and the other men got to dip their wicks or get toasted inside the bar. He liked old Hitch, but dangit! He was strict as a school marm, and Levi had never cared much for schoolin'.

"Okay, duly noted," Orr said. "Hitch, you're in charge while we're gone, okay? I want guards set up around the herd... we're too close to the stock pens to lose any more cattle to rustlers. We're gonna head into town for a few hours but should be back no later than 10:00. If there's any trouble, you send someone in to let us know, alright?"

Hitch nodded, and Jack followed Tom and Mateo into the tiny town for a hot bath and a good meal. As promised, Tom bypassed the Longhorn Round-Up saloon and headed straight for one of the bathhouses for a good wash.

Tom and Mateo followed but the tiny Chinese man who ran the first establishment they came to said, "You two go next door. My wife and daughter have good bath —this place too busy now!"

Obediently, they headed next door and stepped inside. Steam billowed in fragrant clouds, and two sets of feminine hands came out of nowhere and pulled the men toward the back of the adobe building. They were led to large tubs brimming over with hot water. The smell of jasmine and lye stung the men's nostrils as they shed their filthy clothes and stepped into the water.

Sitting down, Jack could hear Mateo sigh with satisfaction and then give out a little yelp. Then, he himself, jolted in surprise as a chubby and smiling young Celestial lady rubbed a soapy rag over his back, shoulders and then down to his groin area. Jack grew instantly hard and blushed. He knew that the Orientals thought nothing of human sexuality and felt no shame in the "human" condition. Jack, however, was raised by starchier people with "Victorian" principles firmly intact.

That intrusive rag, despite his embarrassment, continued on its journey and Jack was able to relax as weeks' worth of dust, sweat and grime was washed away. The girl and her mother tweeted and chirped the whole time they were washing their cowboys and at one point, both Jack and Mateo were hauled up out of the water and onto low stools.

Once there, the razors came out and Jack's itchy whiskers were peeled off like fuzz from a peach. Finally, fresh clothes (their own, but now pounded free of dust) were brought in. Feeling as relaxed as limp noodles, Jack and Mateo paid for the fine service and staggered outside to meet up with their boss.

Tom looked as limp and flushed as his hired men and grinned when he said, "Did you like your baths?"

Jack said, "About peed myself when that little Celestial grabbed my handle, but yes, my bath was very fine."

Mateo added, "Did you have the same experience, Patron?"

Tom looked appalled. "Why, no sir! There was nuthin' but men in my bath and no… they did not grab my bean!"

The men broke into gales of laughter and made their way to a restaurant. Stepping inside, the smell of good food made their mouths water, and after looking at a chalk board menu, they ordered lamb stew, fresh oven biscuits and apple pie for dessert.

They ate their fill and afterward, belched their

contentment with strong, black coffee. Tom asked, "Want to head over to that saloon now... the Deadfall?"

Jack and Mateo agreed, and Mateo said, "I wonder if they sell mezcal, my favorite?"

"Guess we'll find out. Let's go," Tom said.

They had just stepped out of the restaurant when they heard a pistol-shot and a woman's scream. They looked up the street and sure enough, they saw the thin frame of a frail-looking man brandishing a pistol in the air and screaming bloody murder.

Moving closer, they saw Doc Holiday trying to take aim at some poor cowboy who was lying in the street and crawling away from his wrath. The only thing stopping Holiday from shooting the man in the back was Wyatt Earp, who was holding Doc's shooting arm down and trying to pluck the pistol from his hand.

"Let go, dangit!" Doc hiccupped. "Why, you heard him, Wyatt. He called me a cheat! That is no way to talk to a man of good breeding like me, and I aim to put his sorry carcass in the ground!"

Wyatt held on for dear life, however, saying, "You gotta stop this kind of behavior, Doc! Let me have that six-shooter!"

Finally, Jack and his companions saw a big, rather plain woman step outside the bar's bat-wing doors and take Doc's other arm. They couldn't hear what she whispered in his ear, but finally, he stopped struggling and let out a boozy laugh as the wounded cowboy crawled away down the street like a worm.

Chapter Forty-Three

─────────────

THE NEXT MORNING DAWNED COOL AND MISTY. TOM WAS grinning from ear to ear, glad to have made the long haul from Bandera more or less intact and more than happy to know, with Con's ill-gotten booty, he would not only break-even but show a profit.

Jack, on the other hand, was annoyed. He was sitting in back of the Nighthawker's wagon, hiding away under the damp canvas like a scared little church mouse. If it were up to him, he would have ridden into Dodge City on his horse, head held high and ready to face those Blue Sash peckers with authority.

Tom had spoken, though, and Jack was still being paid to follow orders—whether he liked those orders or not. *Anyway,* he sighed in disgust, *Orr is probably right. For all I know, those old guerilla fighters could be camped just outside of Dodge City, ready to start blasting away as soon as they spot me!*

Mateo was driving the wagon, and just ahead of them, Jack could see Con's glowering face staring out the back of Hitch's cook wagon. He'd gotten a little better the last couple of days and according to Hitch, his fever had finally let loose its hold. But with returning health the man gazed from his spot in back of the wagon with bleak and hateful eyes. All the cowboys avoided him now—even those who did not know that he and his dead brother were cattle thieves.

Con's eyes were locked on his face, and the man's phony but sunny smile had been replaced by a look so evil and full of spit it was a wonder Jack didn't melt from the heat of Con's focused rage.

Staring past Hitch's wagon, Jack could see two trains in the near distance spewing black, sooty smoke from their stacks and hear cattle bawling in a steady drone. Squinting, he could make out what seemed like miles of barbed-wire enclosures and men as busy as ants scurrying to and fro amongst the fray.

Just beyond the milling beasts, Jack saw several wooden buildings, a number of big tents, two smithies and one church steeple. A little further, on the other side of the street, he saw several bars, cafes, a big, fancy hotel and much more.

It had been years since he'd ridden through Dodge City, and it had tripled in size. Shaking his head, Jack sat back on his cot and finished packing his things into his saddlebags. He would stay the next day or so, but as soon as things settled, and he was paid what was owed, he planned on heading north—maybe up to Deadwood to look for gold or maybe just do some teamster work. Shotgun for hire, maybe…

Tom Orr appeared at the back of the wagon and spoke, "As soon as we can get this herd separated out and penned in, you and I will go talk to the law in town, okay? Meanwhile, I want the wagons pulled up close to the sheriff's office, hopefully hand Con over, and tell Sheriff Masterson what those old pals of yours have planned."

Jack scowled. "Tom, I never rode with those Blue Sash boys—never! In fact, they killed my girlfriend and her family and ended up burning over 180 folks in Lawrence! That's why I fled, okay?"

Tom, who had tried to make a little joke, but failed, nodded. "Yup, Jack. I'm sorry. Did not mean to ruffle your tail feathers. My wife is forever telling me to stop tryin' to be funny, cuz I just make a hash of it! I know you're a man of honor and wouldn't have played a part in those doings."

"Anyway," Tom continued, "I know it goes against your natural tendencies, but I want you to stay put! Most of the business end of things won't take place until tomorrow, so you shouldn't have to wait long. Can you do that for me, Jack?"

Jack sighed in frustration but nodded. "Yes, boss, I'll wait for you. But what's keeping Con in the wagon? Aren't you afraid he might take off?"

Tom smiled. "I told him that I'd be back with his pay right away. I don't think he's goin' anywhere until he's paid. Won't he be in for a surprise?"

Jack just hoped that Tom would make it quick. Once Con realised all his dough was missing, as well as what his brother had stashed—well, fireworks may happen sooner rather than later!

After about twenty minutes Tom and his herd entered the outskirts of Dodge City. The smell was rank—wet cow hide and reeking, slimy cow muck mixed with the smell of human sweat and filled the back of the wagon, making Jack sneeze in disgust. He sighed, blew his nose and settled back to watch the people walk by, and there were plenty of them.

Cowboys sauntered here and there, walking pigeon-toed and bow-legged. Banker types, with starchy white shirts and string ties stood in groups, many of them holding sheets of paper as they discussed the sales of beef per pound and assorted shipping orders. Prostitutes strolled along in brightly colored, low-cut dresses, their ample breasts and inked-on beauty marks announcing their occupation as loudly as any billboard.

More than seventy people walked around buying and selling at several booths, and Jack saw that many of the women were prim and proper as could be—walking arm and arm with their very proper husbands, and shooing children in front of them with cultured discipline. Two long-skirted priests strode down the boardwalk, and a gaggle of nuns scurried behind them like a flock of blackbirds.

Jack shook his head in amusement thinking, *this place is really a goin' concern!* Then his eyes fell on something so beautiful, he gasped out loud.

Walking along by herself on a boardwalk, Jack saw a woman holding a parasol up against the rain with one hand and clutching a little paper sack with the other, trying to avoid loose boards under her feet, as well as the catcalls of both cowboys and bankers as she moved along.

Jack would have laughed out loud if someone were to suggest he'd just fallen in love at first sight, but he couldn't help but notice his palms had grown clammy and his heart was beating double-time.

The woman, who he judged to be in her middle to late

twenties, had light brown hair which had been tightly coiffed but now coiled up in the days' moisture, and sprang in boisterous corkscrew curls framing a thin but beautiful face.

Her skin was as pale and creamy as buttermilk, except for her finely-wrought nose which was a fiery red and seemed to be peeling from sunburn. Her eyes tilted up at the outer edges and were shadowed by thick, dark eyelashes. He couldn't see the color of those orbs, but he admired how her dark brows slanted across her forehead and her lips parted to show perfectly straight, white teeth.

Jack noticed that a number of men had stopped to stare at the young woman as she passed by, and he had the irrational but powerful urge to jump out of the wagon and pound their faces in. Then, he saw a corpulent but fairly handsome man in a grey velvet suit and handsome vest walk up to her and grasp her shoulder in a gruff manner.

Jack frowned as the man squeezed her arm possessively and dragged her up the boardwalk toward the hotel as she winced and tried to hold her head up but failed to mask her discomfort.

"Hey, mister, go easy on the gal, why don'tcha?" Jack heard a man shout and watched as the man and woman stopped at the front door of the hotel where the ruffian with fine clothing pushed the woman inside so briskly her heels left the floorboards, and Jack gritted his teeth in fury.

Then the lout turned around and shouted in a thick English accent, "This is my wife, gentlemen, and I'll do as I jolly-well please with her. If any man wants to challenge my claim, I'll meet him tomorrow at dawn to settle the matter!"

Jack gave out a soft moan. He'd seen this sort of thing one too many times, and he understood there was not a thing he could do about it. *Dammit!* He swore under his breath as the man who'd challenged the woman's husband slunk away in fear.

Then, Jack saw the young lady's husband slink inside the hotel door, and he abruptly put away his desires and the sudden, powerful longing after a woman to finally get shut of this cattle drive. He was tired of his useless fantasies and meant to ride off alone and unencumbered —as usual.

———

JACK WAITED IMPATIENTLY for about an hour and a half, but true to his word, Tom Orr rode up with a grin. "Just saw the Turnbulls, and it sounds like they've brokered a good deal for my beeves—what's left of them anyway."

Jack smiled. "That's good news, Tom. Congratulation."

Tom peered in at Jack where he sat next to the canvas hoops. "Wouldn't have been able to pull it off without your help, Jack. I'm doubling your bonus, okay?"

Jack's smile grew bigger. "Whal, can't say I'll fight you on that, boss."

Nodding, Tom said, "Well, climb on outta there, why don't you? I want to go see the sheriff and fill 'em in on the situation, and then make it to that big hotel. My wife should be here around three o'clock. Don't aim to be late for that."

Jack clambered out the back of the wagon and saw

Con watching his every move. Despite his courage, Ballard couldn't help but feel a tingle of apprehension run down the back of his neck. He was not afraid of any man or a fair fight—he'd long ago come to terms with the fact that his time on Earth was probably limited.

The Civil War had started his fatalistic viewpoint, not to mention the terrible things that happened to his family and friends before the War of Northern Aggression even began. It didn't help his odds that he often worked as a hired gun, or as a champion to those who were either too poor or too weak to find justice on their own.

But being secretly ambushed or shot in the back by hidden and unknown assassins was another matter—one that had caused him many a sleepless night since he'd grown to manhood. Keeping his hat low, he followed his boss toward the sheriff's office and hoped he and Tom could commission some help from the local law.

As they passed by the back of Hitch's wagon Con snarled, "When do I get paid, Orr?"

Tom said, "Soon! Just hold yer horses for a few more minutes and I'll be back with yer pay."

Con glared silently and sat back on his bed with a grunt.

Stepping inside the sheriff's office, Jack saw a familiar face and his nerves tingled with relief. Bat Masterson sat behind a large desk and grinned as he saw Jack's face. "Why, if it ain't a wayward cowboy! Guess, you boys did okay crossing the reservation, eh?"

"Whal, it was not without a certain amount of... drama," Tom responded. "How do you do? My name's Orr, Tom Orr, out of Bandera, Texas. Pleased to meet ya."

Bat smiled and stuck his hand out to shake. "You the boss of that big drive showed up yesterday?" he asked,

Tom nodded. "Yessir, that would be my herd. My agents have already brokered a deal and we should be outta yer hair within a day or two. Meanwhile, we wanted to talk to you about a situation that's cropped up with one of my men and the threat of assassination against Jack here…"

Masterson frowned. "Assassins—in my town? Over my dead body!"

Jack, Tom and the sheriff of Dodge City sat down and talked for over an hour, and for the first time since Con Drago spilled the beans, Jack was able to breathe.

# Chapter Forty-Four

JACK LAY IN HIS HOTEL BED THE FOLLOWING MORNING AND wasn't aware that his face looked younger, less care-worn than it had in weeks. He was thinking about his and Tom's conversation with Bat Masterson yesterday, and the look of fear and confusion on Con's face as Dodge City's sheriff and deputies arrested him.

He was first confronted at Hitch's cook wagon, then formally accused of cattle rustling, murder and being a destroyer of the peace. Con had startled, and then jumped out of the wagon as if to run but Masterson's deputies 'buffaloed" him—a practice they'd learned from Marshal Earp and his brothers.

Trussed up and howling at the top of his lungs, Con was hauled across the street and into the sheriff's office/ jailhouse while Tom and Jack watched. Just before being man-handled through the door, Con spied Jack and screamed, "Oh, you think you're so smart. Well, don't you worry—I may swing, but you're going down in a hail of bullets. Traitor!"

Then he was gone, and Jack let out the air he'd been holding in his lungs.

Tom sighed, "Well, that's taken care of, anyway. We still gotta watch our backs, but we got those two deputies shadowing us now. Let's head down to the bank and get your money, okay?"

Jack had nodded, more than ready to leave this town, and Orr's cattle drive in his dust. They headed into the bank, and Jack watched as a tall, red-haired woman let out a cry of joy and flew into Tom's arms. Orr and his wife kissed so passionately, Jack looked away and a couple of older women let out squawks of scandalized outrage.

A few minutes later, Jack was introduced to Evangeline Orr, and handed an astounding amount of money. Embarrassed, Jack tried to give some of the notes back, but Mrs. Orr said, "Nonsense, Jack. My Tom has told me what you did to help him and the herd, and we thank you from the bottom of our hearts."

Jack smiled at her and shook Tom Orr's hand. "Do you need me to stick around, Tom? Maybe help you separate out the herd?"

Tom shook his head. "Nah, my hands will take care of it. One thing, though, before you go. Mateo wants to talk to you. I've already said yes to him, but it's up to you, of course."

"What is?" jack asked.

Tom shrugged and replied, "He'll tell you when he's ready, I reckon. Say, if'n you're in need of work in the future, we can always use a good hand on the ranch. I probably won't attempt another drive like this one—at least not for a while, but if I do, please leave me an address where I can contact you, okay?"

Jack had nodded and said goodbye and good luck, then took some of his new cash and his saddlebags to the same hotel the pretty girl and her husband were staying at for a good meal and a bed that didn't move, jolt and shudder with constant travel.

Now he stared up at the ceiling and thought about taking a train up north. He could travel by horse, for sure, but he was hip-sore and tired of rough travel. Always about half-broke and loath to part with what little money he possessed, he weighed the price of a train ticket and wondered if it was a foolish waste of money or a luxury he could finally afford.

Hopping out of bed, he decided to go down to the hotel's stable and fetch Rebel. He would make a quick trip out to the herd to find Mateo, wish his new friends—like Hitch, young Levi and Latigo—farewell and then go see about the price of a train ticket to Idaho before eating some chow at a café.

He walked down the staircase and glanced to his left into the hotel dining room. It was filled to bursting with customers and Jack could smell sausage gravy and strong coffee in the air. He could also see the beautiful girl's rotten husband holding court at one of the center tables.

His toney English accent reverberated off the walls and Jack itched to smack the self-satisfied smirk off the cad's fat face. He shrugged though, knowing that the man and his wife were none of his beeswax and the sooner he stopped thinking about them the better it would be for all concerned.

Jack marched past the crowd to the front desk in order to pay for his room, and heard a man say, "But, Count,

Longhorns are hardier, and not as prone to tick fever as Herefords—that's why we use them in the big drives!"

The "Count" answered with a guffaw of scorn. "Why, Longhorn meat is as tough as my boot. Give me Hereford meat any day, I say!"

*An English count! Oh, for pity's sake,* Jack thought, *no wonder he's as arrogant as Old Georgie!* Disgusted, he rolled his eyes and the man behind the counter grinned. "Not impressed?" he whispered.

Jack shook his head. "No."

The man replied, "Well, Sir Abernathy's a *royal* pain in *our* asses, that's fer sure. Can't wait until he leaves tomorrow. I swear, the sounds coming from his and the Mrs. room every night would curdle your milk!" He continued to whisper and glared with loathing in Abernathy's direction—safely concealed by Jack's broad shoulders.

Jack sighed and paid his bill. Then he walked through the back door toward the stable. He saw Rebel raise his head with a large chunk of hay dangling from his mouth and heard the sound of a woman's soft sobs.

Stopping in mid-stride, Jack peered over a fence rail and saw the girl of his dreams spreading liniment over the flanks of a very fine, black gelding. Jack winced at the amount of damage done to the horse's rump and wondered who in their right mind would set-to so savagely that many of the cuts were over an inch deep!

The horse trembled at Mrs. Abernathy's touch although Jack could see that she was being as gentle as possible. She was whispering, "Shush, that's it. We'll get you fixed up, my darling. I'm so sorry about what he did to you... shush."

Jack suddenly knew, without a shadow of doubt, that

Abernathy had beaten this horse to the point of sick shock and possibly permanent injury sometime in the last day or two. The cuts were still fresh and drops of blood welled-up at the woman's gentlest touch.

"Can I help you, ma'am?" he whispered, and the young woman jumped with a gasp.

Turning toward him, Jack saw her reddened but gorgeous gray eyes, her sunburned nose and a large, livid bruise on her left cheek. The horse was, obviously, not the only creature suffering under Count Abernathy's abuse.

She blushed and said, "Oh, you startled me!" then she took a breath and asked, "Yes, please. I'm trying to help my horse-which was injured—but he's in so much pain, he won't stand still!"

Jack went around the front of the horse to hold its halter while the woman tended to its wounds. "My name's Jack Ballard, ma'am. What's yours?"

The girl blushed and said, "My name is Madeline Abernathy, and this is my pride and joy, Prince. We're pleased to make your acquaintance."

Jack heard her American accent and despite every sensible thought in his noggin, was suddenly head over heels in love.

Madeline looked past Jack's shoulder to see if anyone was headed their way and then whispered, "We must hurry. I don't want my…" her mouth twisted with sorrow, "… my husband to see what I'm doing."

Jack answered, "We'll finish this soon, but you know that this horse may no longer be fit to ride?"

She nodded. "Yes, sir, I do know it. Sadly."

The young lady smeared the rest of the ointment over the horse's rear and tossed the empty pot away in a nearby rubbish bin. "The only time I could break away to buy this medicine from the veterinarian was yesterday, while Martin was gone. I thought I had enough time to buy the lineament, but my husband caught me, and punished me for leaving the hotel room."

"Why did he beat this horse, do you know?" Jack asked.

Madeline trembled, and her voice quivered in anger as she answered Jack's question. "This is my own horse. I think Martin beat him just to hurt me."

"It's okay, ma'am. A horse can take a pretty good licking and still be loyal to those that love it and treat it kindly. He knows that you weren't responsible for the beating he got. Still, it would be best if you kept him isolated from other animals and far away from the man who beat it in the first place."

She nodded silently and placed a warming blanket over the horse's back. Then, they both heard Abernathy's voice heading their way. Looking up at him, Madeline said, "Please! You must not be seen helping me and Prince or we'll both suffer the consequences!"

Jack nodded and stepped away to fetch his saddlebags. Suddenly, a shot rang out and he heard Madeline cry out in pain. Staring in shock, Jack watched as the lovely young woman sank to the ground clutching her left arm. Looking up at him, she whispered, "Mr. Ballard, I think I've been shot."

## Chapter Forty-Five

JACK FOUND HIMSELF FROZEN IN SHOCK. *BUSHWHACKED!* HE thought, but his first instinct was to help Madeline. He dropped to his knees and started to crab his way toward the injured woman but suddenly, her horse let out an unearthly groan, fell to its knees and then tipped over dead, narrowly missing the woman's outstretched legs.

Jack realized that, somehow, the rifle shot had hit Prince instead of his own person. Madeline's gunshot wound had either been the result of the slug's passage or a ricochet. Regardless, the girl was shot, and Jack meant to see her safe from harm before he went outside to face his enemies.

He had just crawled to Madeline's side when a belligerent English voice cried out, "Wot in bloody hell is going on? You there... what are you doing with my wife? Bugger off, or I'll see you horse-whipped!"

Jack ignored Abernathy for the moment and stared into Madeline's lovely gray eyes. "Where are you hurt, ma'am?"

Madeline shuddered. "I'm fine—really. It's just a scrape on my arm but... but they shot my Prince!"

She burst into fresh tears at seeing her dead horse lying only inches away from her leg. But then Abernathy was on top of them and put his hands—on Jack's shoulders in order to pull him off his wife.

Unfortunately, the count didn't have enough common sense to think hard about accosting an American ex-soldier. As Abernathy pulled Jack forward to give him a piece of his mind, he came face to face with the biggest pistol he'd ever seen.

Jack's .44-40 Colt came to rest on the tip of Abernathy's nose, and the English blue-blood almost peed himself when the cowboy hissed, "Listen up, mister..."

Abernathy, unable to contain himself despite the enormous gun squashing his nose flat whispered, "Count, sir... I'm am the Count of Brisbane..."

Jack glared. "I don't care if you're the King of Siam, buddy. You need to get your wife outta here and seek medical attention for her wound. She's been shot by assassins and I don't think they're done yet. So, git!"

Jack released the man, who glanced about with scared eyes before bending over to help his wife to her feet. Then, he paused on his way into the hotel's back entrance and snarled, "If my wife is seriously injured because of what you might have done to come under fire, then you'll be hearing from my second!"

"Whatever you like, *mister.*" Jack said. "Better scuttle off though, the next bullet may hit you."

Martin Abernathy did just that, squeezing his wife's uninjured shoulder so hard she cried out in pain. "How now, wife," he whispered malevolently "why were you down in the stable when I specifically told you to stay in our room?"

Madeline said nothing as Martin whisked her into the hotel proper. The desk clerk, who had heard the gunplay just outside the front door, was standing behind his counter with a loaded shotgun. Seeing Madeline and the blood running through her fingers on her upper left-arm, he cried, "Doc! Doctor Williams, there's an injured woman here needs your attention."

An elderly gentleman scurried over to tend to Madeline's arm, as Abernathy stepped back in disgust. He hadn't planned on seeking medical attention for his wife, figuring he could patch her up just fine by himself. (Also, he knew that his behavior toward his spouse would not hold up to medical scrutiny, and he wanted to avoid that kind of scandal, if possible, at least until they hit Missoula, Montana and Madeline's family ranch.)

Still, he was licked, for now, and watched as the old man dipped into his medical kit for alcohol and bandages. Suddenly, a roar of gunfire filled the air, and those folks still inside the restaurant screamed and ducked for cover.

———

HITCH, Levi and Mateo had ridden into town for some grub and to catch Jack Ballard before he up and left town. They were sitting on a bench outside the milliner's shop across the street from the hotel, when they saw five armed men walking side by side up Main Street. "Watch out, boys…" Hitch murmured. "I think it's time to make ourselves scarce."

The three cowboys stood and scurried to their left to

hide behind a pile of fresh lumber next to a solicitor's office. Huddling together, they saw one man wearing a blue silk sash instead of a belt lift his rifle and shoot into the hotel's stable area.

They then heard a feminine cry and the sound of something heavy hitting the ground. "Well, I swear, they just shot themselves a girl!" he growled.

Mateo pulled his pistol from his gun belt. "I think I hear Senor Jack as well, Mr. Hitch. I must go help, if I can!"

Hitch shook his head. "No! You stay put for a minute. Let's see how this plays out before you charge in and get yourself drilled. There's five o' them and only two of us who're any good with a firearm!"

"I can shoot, if you just let me try!" Levi whispered.

But Hitch hissed, "You shut-up, sprout. I don't aim to see you six-feet-under, unless I put you there my own self!"

Levi glowered, but stayed put as ordered.

The three men watched as one of the five shooters hollered, "Jack Ballard, come out and be tried by a jury of your peers, who have found you guilty of treason!"

Silence reigned, however, and Mateo again threatened to leave and fight. "I must go and help Senor Ballard!" he whispered, and Hitch tried to stop him when another voice filled the air.

"I am not a traitor!" Jack shouted. "I have never betrayed my country or my countrymen. It is *you* who took matters into your own hands and fired Lawrence, Kansas, killing over 180 good citizens in your insane lust for power!"

The five gunmen looked at each other, and the same

man who'd shot into the stable yelled, "Well, Jack, I guess we must agree to disagree. Step out here, and we'll settle this once and for all!"

Hitch peered about and saw at least a dozen citizens huddled behind their own makeshift hiding places. He also heard many of them grumble and growl at what Jack had just said. There were not many folks in Dodge City who had not been negatively impacted by the Lawrence massacre, and for some, those old wounds were still as fresh and painful as ever.

None of those people knew Jack Ballard, at least Hitch didn't think so, but many of them recognized the blue sash two of the shooters wore. Most Kansas natives knew all about the Blue Sash society and Quantrill's Raiders and understood that many of those men were, or had been, close-way too close—to some of the most notorious outlaws in the American west.

Hitch grinned as he saw two men suddenly pluck guns from their saddle-bags and spied one man rooting around in his wife's handbag, of all things, and coming up with an enormous six-shooter.

*Well,* Hitch Potter thought, *I guess we're all in for a howdy-do!*

Then, a new voice pierced the air. "Hold yer hands up! You are all in clear violations of the Guns and Ordinance Act of Dodge City! Put yer weapons away, or we'll shoot you down like the dirty dogs you are!"

Bat Masterson, Virgil and Wyatt Earp and several deputies had appeared out of nowhere and now stood, armed to the teeth, on both sides of Main Street.

## Chapter Forty-Six

HITCH WATCHED AS THE SHOULDERS OF THE GUNMEN drooped at the realization they were surrounded by the local law. Three of the men stooped and placed their rifles on the ground and, for a moment, Hitch thought the situation would resolve itself peacefully.

But the lead man with the blue sash lifted his rifle once more and shot into the interior of the stable. He was instantly filled with holes as the sheriff, the town marshal and all their deputies commenced enforcing the law. One of the other gunners was hit as well, but he fell to the ground very much alive and howling in pain. "God dammit" he cried, "I'm gut-shot, boys! That there sheriff done me in, for sure!"

The other three men, seeing that a gunfight was the only way out, pulled pistols out of their rigs and started blasting away at the stable, the lawdogs and even the townsfolks who were fighting back with guns of their own.

Hitch pulled Levi away from the action whizzing by them and said, "You stay put, hear?"

Levi, who had never even seen a gunfight, much less been an active participant in one, nodded and scurried backward out of sight. Then Hitch said to Mateo, "Well, here's your chance, sonny. If this keeps up, Jack will take a bullet, just 'cuz he's trapped inside that stable. Let's add a little pepper to this mix, eh?"

Mateo grinned and said, "Si, senor. You take care now!" And then he ran left and planted himself behind a handy horse trough. Once there, he took careful aim and hit one of the active shooters in the upper thigh.

Blue sash fluttering, the man toppled over, screaming, and his two companions ran over to where he lay in the dirt. "Go! Go get that son of a bitch!" he hollered, and the men began to crawl on their hands and knees toward the stable doors. But, one by one, Bat Masterson, Virgil Earp and his brother, Wyatt, shot the men dead.

Silence ensued, and folks looked around to take stock of the situation. Two of the shooters were still alive—the man Masterson and his deputies had shot and the man with the blue sash who lay writing in pain in the dust.

Hitch walked over and looking down saw a middle-aged man bleeding out from a gunshot would to his thigh. Looked to him like the bullet had nicked the femoral artery and this blue-sashed feller was breathing his last. Just as the town doc and the mortician showed up, Hitch searched the now crowded street, trying to spot Jack Ballard.

Looking high and low, Hitch couldn't see Ballard anywhere. Then, his own warning came back to him, and he took off running toward the stable. He cleared the door and stopped to let his eyes adjust. Then, he heard Jack say, "Over here, Hitch."

Someone stepped past him, and Hitch startled slightly but saw that Virgil and Wyatt Earp were now hunched over and trying to help Ballard who was on the floor and leaning back against a stall door, his whole body drenched in blood. Heart pounding in dread, Hitch saw that Jack had caught a bullet in the chest. Fearing the worst, he said, "Jack, how're doin?"

Jack grinned and then grimaced. "It's a through and through, I'm thinking. Bullets right here, behind me in the wood." Then he lost color and started gasping for air.

"Go fetch the doc!" Wyatt shouted, and Hitch took off running again. He found the town doc just placing a blanket over the blue sash man's body and grabbed the doctor's arm. "Hurry! There's a good man bleeding to death in the stable!" The doc grabbed his bag and followed Hitch into the stable where Jack lie passed out against a stall door.

He looked quite blue from where Hitch stood, but Jack stirred when the doc bent down and applied clean bandages against the gunshot wound. Doctor Williams said, "This man is drowning in his own blood! I'm going to lean him forward and I want you…" pointing to Virgil, "to place the compress against his back. Press hard when you do."

Doc Williams and the Earp brothers leaned Jack forward as he groaned against the agony, but immediately his color returned. The cloud of shock lifted from Ballard's eyes and he grinned up at Hitch. "I sure could use some of that laudy about now…"

Hitch was more than eager to comply, but Williams

held up his hand. "No! Not yet, anyway. Let's see if we can lean him back first and how far the shock is gonna go before we drug him."

Virgil and Wyatt gently pushed Jack back against the door and he kept his color. Grimacing, he said, "Whal—if hurtin' like hell indicates anything, I think I'm gonna live."

The doctor said, "Yup, reckon so. The bullet missed your right lung but tore through a lot of muscles and tendons. You'll survive if infection doesn't set in, but you're gonna have to lay low for a while to let your body regain its strength."

Jack frowned. "How long?"

Williams shrugged. "Hard to say, really. You are still a young man and seem strong enough, but I'd say you're bed-ridden for, at least, a month."

Disgruntled, Jack closed his eyes for a quick snooze but didn't wake up for two days.

————

JACK CAME TO SLOWLY AND, at first, thought he was in a busy, riotous saloon. There was a babble of voices and a piano in the background tinkling away. Then, he realized that he was in a bed and his friends were speaking together quietly. The tinkling was actually the sound of hammers striking nail heads. He listened to the conversation for a few moments before opening his eyes.

"... Doc says he's gonna make it, but it'll be months before he can live normally—without pain."

"Whal, he's a tough man... Doc don't know him."

"Hey, that was a rifle slug plowed through his upper torso—it's a wonder he's still breathin'."

Suddenly, Jack focused on his wounded chest and almost gasped out loud. The pain was unbelievable, pulsing in agonizing waves—at once sharp like broken glass and hot, like live flames.

He wanted to weep with self-pity but took himself firmly in hand knowing that giving into weakness now was a sure-fire way to sabotage his body's ability to heal. Gritting his teeth, Jack opened his eyes and saw Tom Orr, Hitch and Mateo sitting on hard, wooden chairs along the far wall.

Jack tried to say howdy, but his voice failed him, and he let out a sick—sounding croak. The men glanced his way and smiling, Tom said, "Welcome back to the land of the living, Jack."

Clearing his throat, Jack rasped, "Glad to be back... how long have I been out?"

Hitch said, "Been two days but the doc says you're out of the woods now."

Jack smiled at the men, realizing that although he'd only known them about six weeks, their faces had become dear. Girlish tears threatened, but he blinked them away in disgust and said, "What are you guys doing hangin' around here? Shouldn't you be getting back home?"

Tom nodded, "Yessir, Jack. It's time for us to head home. We were just waiting until you pulled through the worst of it."

"Don't worry, I'll survive," Jack murmured.

"We know you will, partner. We just wanted to make sure of that, and wish you farewell," Tom agreed then added, "We already talked to the law around here and we-all of us—are acquitted of any wrong-doing. The Blue Sash boys... that's a different story."

Jack asked, "How's that?"

Hitch took over talking and told Jack that Con, and another man named William Branson had survived the shoot-out but were to hang in a weeks' time. All the other men seeking vengeance against Jack's so-called traitorous actions had been killed during the dust-up two days earlier.

"It was suicide, Jack. Plain and simple. Those boys were completely surrounded and out gunned ten-to-one. Still they died trying to put you down, and now they're nuthin' but dust!"

Hitch's eyes sparkled, and Jack thought the old man was probably already writing about what had happened in his beloved journals.

Tom grinned. "Anyhow, me and the Mrs. are leaving on a coach in about an hour. Hitch and the rest of my ranch hands will follow us back to Bandera with the gear and wagons. Nice thing, though, they'll have an Army escort, at least for the first hundred miles or so."

Then he and Hitch got up from their chairs and walked over to Jack's bed. Sticking their hands out to shake, both Tom Orr and his hired man, Hitch Potter, wished him a fond farewell and told him to come south to the Triple T ranch if he ever found himself short on work and out of cash.

Jack said goodbye and good luck, and watched as they walked out the door, headed back home to Bandera, Texas. Then, his eyes closed for a moment, but he heard a soft voice say, "Senor Jack? May I speak with you for un momento, por favor?"

Jack's eyelids popped open. He had forgotten that

Mateo was also in the room. Turning his head, Ballard said, "Sure, Mateo. What do you need?"

Mateo's lovely olive complexion turned pink and he squirmed in embarrassment. Jack, watching the startling transformation said, "Hey kid, there's nothing you can say that will change my good opinion of you, okay? Just relax and tell me what you need."

Mateo looked into Jack's eyes and said, "Senor, may I ride with you for a while? I admire you and there is much I can learn from you. I don't ask for you to be my patron, but a partner. I think you could use help at this time, and I offer my services freely. You helped me—saved my life! Now, I want to repay your kindness."

Jack, being ever the loner, almost said no. But he stopped and reconsidered. He was wounded—badly—of that he was certain. He knew that he could really use the help and he saw great potential and honor in the handsome young face before him.

Maybe, if they started out as equals, their partnership could blossom into a real friendship—something Jack finally understood he needed-desperately.

Jack smiled then, and said, "Partners? Heck yeah."

## Epilogue

SEVEN WEEKS HAD PASSED, AND JACK WAS FINALLY ABLE TO walk to the town stables to visit with Rebel without gasping in pain and falling into bed afterwards from bone-deep weakness and fatigue.

Mateo was a great help to him during those first few weeks of recovery. He did all the shopping and brought café-bought meals to the little boarding house room he'd rented. He changed Jack's dressing, and learned how to play poker and chess, while Jack enjoyed the chance to win—for once.

He had also seen Con Drago hang along with one of the Blue Sash boys. There was quite a crowd, Mateo said, but he didn't stick around for the picnic that followed.

Jack was now sitting on a park bench and looking about at Dodge City and its citizens. Mateo had taken their horses to the northbound train, and he and Jack would be hitting the rails in a little under an hour. They were headed to Missoula, Montana Territory.

Jack cringed, knowing that he was following his heart,

although he'd told Mateo there was plenty of work to be found there—which was, apparently, also the truth.

He remembered the last time he'd seen Madeline Abernathy. It was about two weeks after he'd been shot, and she had managed to sneak away from her husband long enough to say goodbye before they left for Montana.

She was as lovely as ever but still so terribly sad, Jack's heart pinched in his chest. She had told him that when she was eighteen-years-old, her mother had insisted that she and her lady's companion, Betty Gibbons, should tour the "Continent". Madeline's mother, Adele Fitzsimmons, was nothing if not a high-brow, and thought it was the right of every young lady of good-breeding.

At first, Madeline was dancing on air—she was well-received at both the English and French courts and her dance-card was filled to capacity every night. Then, Count Abernathy had made an appearance.

She thought, in the beginning, that he was the perfect suitor. Handsome, a good conversationalist, a better than average horseman, well-versed in running a farm and animal husbandry, and a *Royal*—to boot! Her mother was ecstatic. Her daughter would be a countess! And, she wasted no time telling her friends and neighbors all about Madeline's elevated status.

The marriage was whirlwind affair and for a while, Martin behaved himself. But it soon became clear that he was a booze-hound, a womanizer, a wastrel, and flat-broke. In fact, there were so many English lenders petitioning him for payment, Martin was close to having to spend the rest of his life in debtor's prison.

He had wooed the American heiress for her money, but secretly despised her, thinking she and her family were as common as dirt. Their transatlantic crossing was a nightmarish affair in which Martin cruised the ships dining rooms and gambling halls making a fool of himself, while Madeline and Betty huddled together in their berth trying to avoid his sudden fits of anger and flying fists.

Madeline told Jack that they had only been stateside for about two months and had spent much of it here in Dodge City figuring out a way to transport the only thing of value Martin had brought into the marriage… one hundred head of English, Herefords.

They intended to bring the herd up by train, as even Martin was forced to admit that his cattle were not nearly as hardy as Longhorns and might very well perish on an extended over-land journey north.

"We're leaving in two hours," she had said, and her eyes were damp with unshed tears. "Jack, I don't hardly know you and please forgive my boldness, but I wish I'd met you before… before I threw my hat in with that scallywag. I'm afraid he'll be the life of me!"

Jack had managed to get to his feet and give the young lady a hug. Wishing her well, he added, "Well, you never know… I might just show up one of these days."

He didn't know why he'd said it, but as her eyes focused on his with hope and gratitude, he knew he would move heaven and earth to make sure Madeline Fitzsimmons stayed safe.

Now, as Jack watched his young friend Mateo walking his way he smiled, and thought, "How life does change."

Then, he stood up and joined Mateo for a long train ride north to Montana.

## A Look At Deadman's Lament

BY LINELL JEPPSEN

The year is 1872. Twelve-year-old Matthew Wilcox leads a charmed life on his family's sprawling ranch in Washington Territory until a series of tragic events leave him orphaned and in the clutches of a vicious band of outlaws. Threatened by the gang leader's perverted cousin, Top Hat, Matthew also faces Indian attacks, dangerous wildlife, and a deadly snowstorm. He survives but burns with an overwhelming hunger for revenge.

Thirteen years later, Matthew - now a Spokane County sheriff - realizes that Top Hat is riding again with a new gang called the Mad Hatters. It means risking his friends, his family and the love of a good woman, but Matthew must find the man who destroyed what he once loved most in the world. To that end, he and his posse venture into Idaho gold country to capture the Mad Hatters.

Top Hat, however, has a different idea. He turns the tables, heading to the sheriff's hometown of Granville and going after everyone Matthew holds dear.

What follows will haunt Sheriff Wilcox for the rest of his life as he confronts the hatred, vengeance and retribution buried deep in his own soul. Matthew will do anything, though, to put an end to A DEADMAN'S LAMENT.

*AVAILABLE NOW ON AMAZON*

# About The Authors

LINELL JEPPSEN

**Linell Jeppsen** is a writer of science fiction and fantasy. Her vampire novel, *Detour to Dusk*, has received over 44-four and five star reviews. Her novel *Story Time*, with over 130 4-and 5-star reviews, is a science fiction post-apocalyptic novel, and has been touted by the Paranormal Romance Guild, Sandy's Blog Spot, Coffee time Romance, Bitten by Books and 64 top reviewers as a five-star read, filled with terror, love, loss, and the indomitable beauty and strength of the human spirit. *Story Time* was also nominated as the best new read of 2011 by the PRG. Her dark fantasy novel, *Onio* (a story about a half-human Sasquatch who falls in love with a human girl), was released in December 2012 and won 3rd place as the best fantasy romance of 2012 by the PRG reviewers guild. Her novel, *The War of Odds*, won the IBD award for fantasy fiction and boasts 18 5-star reviews since its release in February of 2013. It also placed 2nd, as the best YA paranormal book of 2013 by the PRG.

# About The Authors

JEB ROSEBROOK

Journalist and novelist, **Jeb Rosebrook** was best known for his writing credits in film and television including the Sam Peckinpah film "Junior Bonner" starring Steve McQueen and Disney's "The Black Hole". He was nominated for two Writers' Guild of America television writing awards and an Emmy as co-writer of "I Will Fight No More Forever", the story of Chief Joseph. Film credits include the Sam Peckinpah directed classic, *Junior Bonner*, starring Steve McQueen and Disney's iconic sci-fi classic *The Black Hole*. Television credits for writing and co-writing and producing include numerous television films and mini-series, including Kenny Roger's *The Gambler*, *The Yellow Rose* and *The Outsiders*.

Jeb lived with his wife Dorothy in Scottsdale, Arizona until he passed away in August 2018.